P9-BIH-234

The
Bug Boys

The
Bug Boys

Stewart Hoffman

THE BUG BOYS

Copyright © 2016 Stewart Hoffman.

All rights reserved. No part of this book may be used or reproduced by any means, graphic, electronic, or mechanical, including photocopying, recording, taping or by any information storage retrieval system without the written permission of the author except in the case of brief quotations embodied in critical articles and reviews.

This is a work of fiction. All of the characters, names, incidents, organizations, and dialogue in this novel are either the products of the author's imagination or are used fictitiously.

iUniverse books may be ordered through booksellers or by contacting:

iUniverse
1663 Liberty Drive
Bloomington, IN 47403
www.iuniverse.com
1-800-Authors (1-800-288-4677)

Because of the dynamic nature of the Internet, any web addresses or links contained in this book may have changed since publication and may no longer be valid. The views expressed in this work are solely those of the author and do not necessarily reflect the views of the publisher, and the publisher hereby disclaims any responsibility for them.

Any people depicted in stock imagery provided by Thinkstock are models, and such images are being used for illustrative purposes only. Certain stock imagery © Thinkstock.

ISBN: 978-1-5320-0344-8 (sc)
ISBN: 978-1-5320-0345-5 (e)

Library of Congress Control Number: 2016912071

Print information available on the last page.

iUniverse rev. date: 10/12/2016

Contents

For
Anne S. Gillespie

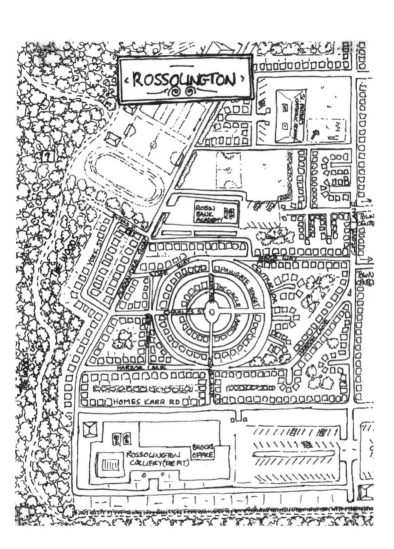

CHAPTER 1

Wake Up Call

It was Monday, and Alex awoke to the sound of his dad peeing. It was 6:30 a.m. exactly. Alex didn't have to look at his alarm clock, or even turn it off. His father was that reliable, and loud.

Alex's tiny bedroom was right next to the modest semi-detached home's only toilet, so he was mindful to close his door before going to bed. The sound of wee splashing into the toilet water was bad enough, but it was nothing compared to what usually followed.

FART! And there it was. The morning's release, ushering in the new day with an explosion of methane, built up by his dad's intestinal tract as it worked through the night on his diet of fast food and soda pop. A sound akin to a car tire exploding, combined with a noise you'd expect a dying duck to make. Alex smiled as he heard his two younger brothers, Graham and Robert, giggle in their room across the hall.

"Frank Adams!" complained Alex's mother, Sharon.

"What?"

Alex loved this bizarre family tradition.

After throwing back his solar system themed covers, Alex rolled his short chubby frame out of bed. After opening his curtains to let in the day, he got an unpleasant shock. Overnight, a spider had set up camp on his window, and had successfully built a large web connecting the latch to the frame. The spider waited for its next victim, using the latch for cover. Alex put on his glasses and carefully moved closer to the latch to get a better look. He could just make out the spider's thick body and legs. He hated that kind of spider the most. He could handle the tiny ones, and even the spiders with the long spindly legs and tiny bodies. The big ones, however, were too fast and too unpredictable for his liking.

Across the room, Alex heard a buzzing sound. He looked around but at first couldn't see what was making it—then he located it. A fly had also gotten into his room somehow, and was likely excited to see the light coming from the window. Alex ducked as the fly buzzed past him, and once the little bug reached the window, it repeatedly head-butted the glass looking for a way out.

Alex could see the spider pull back into its corner of the web, ready to pounce if the fly happened to get tangled in its trap. All three players in this morning's drama, didn't have to wait long before the action started. The fly, not looking where it was going, slammed into the spider's web.

The spider wasted no time, and crawled out from its hiding spot. Alex watched as the fly failed to break the sticky grip of the web. It was then overwhelmed by the large arachnid; a few seconds later, it was all over. The fly stopped moving, and the spider began wrapping it up as a present for later.

Alex saw this as an opportunity to let some fresh air into his room. With the spider now preoccupied, he grabbed a pencil and broke the web's connection to the latch. The spider and the wrapped-up fly swung away, and Alex quickly opened his window. A gust of wind pushed into the room, causing the poorly anchored web to flap about. The spider was knocked off its home, landing on the window sill. From there it quickly crawled under the ledge and disappeared behind the bedside cabinet. Alex decided it was a good time to leave his bedroom.

Alex marched into the kitchen, and opened the cabinets underneath the sink. Inside were all the supplies he needed. He grabbed a pair of pink rubber gloves and a large can of bug spray.

"What on earth are you doing?" asked Alex's mum, who was busily setting up breakfast.

"Spider, Mum," he replied as he put on a pair of his dad's safety goggles and an old painters mask. He stood in front of his mother ready to do battle.

"Go get 'em tiger," she said.

Alex charged back to his room to do battle with the spider.

Sharon had perfected and loved her morning routine. The men came first in this household, or at least that's what she'd say to them. Her real objective was to get *her* house all to herself, as quickly as possible. She liked to think she was the calm guiding force getting each day off to the perfect start, stealthily navigating her short oval shaped frame around the house, strategically placing items her boys would need in places she knew they'd eventually be.

As the boys argued upstairs over the bathroom, she was downstairs in her favourite paisley quilted dressing gown, calmly putting their breakfast together—popping toast and arranging cereal choices, along with milk, sugar, jam and marmalade, all while brewing the tea. By the time the males had assembled themselves into some state of readiness for the day ahead, the dining room table was ready to accept them—conditional on whether they passed her morning inspection, of course.

Once the boys were ready, Sharon walked down the line. Frank's collar got adjusted and some stray shaving cream was found slowly sliding down his neck. Alex's school tie looked like the minute and hour hands of a clock (it was 8:20, apparently), so Sharon re-tied it, made the hour hand longer, and set it to point at 6:30. Robert, the youngest Adams, had been known to show up wearing only his favourite red underwear, but today managed to find and wear most of his school uniform. He was, however, sporting mismatched socks, so was sent back upstairs to find a match to either one. Sharon merely glanced at Graham; she knew there'd be nothing to fix there. Graham was a middle-aged tailor trapped inside a nine-year-old's body.

After the inspection was over, Alex grabbed two slices of toast, and headed for the back door.

"Err, excuse me," said Sharon, "where do you think you're going?"

"Round Ian's. We've got a war to finish."

"Really? Couldn't war wait until after school?"

"No, Mum. I've got a new plan of attack I want to try out. It's going to be epic."

Sharon rolled her eyes, already regretting the initial question. "Fine, go on then. Oh, and remember, your dad is driving you home after the school's visit to the pit today."

After breakfast, it was time for the males to go about their day. Robert and Graham grabbed their school bags and walked through the living room to stand by the front door. Frank followed but was stopped by Sharon. "Hold your horses there, Mr. Frank Adams." She pointed to his lunch tin on the kitchen counter.

"I've packed a peanut butter sandwich, and two apples."

Frank couldn't look less excited.

"Please don't throw it away and get burgers with your mates."

Seeing Frank's phony hurt expression, Sharon moved in closer and patted Frank's large belly. "You know the doctor said you should watch what you eat."

With a sigh, Frank nodded and picked up the tin. Sharon then pointed to her cheek, and Frank kissed it. "Okay?"

Frank hesitated.

"Okaaayyyy?"

"Yes, okay," sighed Frank.

From the front door, arms crossed, Sharon watched Frank, Robert and Graham head out into the cool spring air and get into Frank's car parked in the street. Sharon was finally alone, and loved it. This was her favourite part of the day—the quiet after the storm. She poured herself a cup of tea, adding a splash of milk and half a teaspoon of sugar. She took her tea into the living room, carefully inspecting the carpet and furniture as she went, creating her mental to-do list for the day's chores. Some of her bowls of lavender-scented potpourri needed refreshing, and it had been at least two days since she last dusted her collection of decorative ornaments.

Sharon sat down on her favourite recliner and carefully pulled the wooden lever to extend the footrest. She then reached over to the end-table next to her chair, and opened the small drawer at the front. Inside was a black notebook. She picked it up, and unhooked the pen that was clipped to it. Flipping through the book, she stopped on a page half-filled with crossed out numbers. The most recent and untouched number was 825. She crossed that out and wrote 826 next to it.

CHAPTER 2

The Battle Britannica!

There was darkness and peace, followed by light and more war, and the only thing Private Hopkins remembered was joining his battalion on the battlefield for yet another tour of duty.

The same field, with landmarks Hopkins recognized, but arranged differently somehow. Hopkins could see Almanac Point, but he could have sworn it was on the east side of the field the last time he was transported here. There was also a new formation directly north of his position, a large valley he and his team named Britannica Pass. Or had they? When Hopkins really thought about it, he actually couldn't remember who came up with the name. It was something that was just understood. That was Britannica Pass, and it was the most direct and dangerous way to the other side of the field. Hopkins knew this, and had always known this, but it still felt like fresh information somehow.

Other things started to trouble the Private. Why did their commanding officer, Captain Harris, only pack a pair of binoculars? No rifle or pistol as far as Hopkins could see, just a pair of binoculars, which Harris used to scan the horizon looking for enemy troops. *Was this bravery? Or had the man lost his mind*? It certainly seemed to inspire Corporal Smiley, the battalion's radio controller. Again, no weapon but seemingly ready to charge into battle with the battalion's only means of communicating with base command. Hopkins wondered if anyone else knew how to operate the radio.

"Captain Harris, sir, new instructions from command headquarters," Smiley shouted, as he hopped over to Harris to discuss the message. The two men quietly conferred as Hopkins and the rest of the team stared at each other and shrugged. The two officers ended their conversation with a salute, and Captain Harris turned to face the troops. "New orders, men; we're to move six meters north west of our position. Let's hop to it!"

The Captain turned and headed north-west, and was closely shadowed by Smiley. Hopkins and the rest of the team picked up their gear and followed. Six meters. This was the largest move they'd made all day, and Hopkins wondered if the bigwigs back at headquarters were acting on new information. Until this bold step, they had spent the last couple of hours moving a meter here, or a couple of meters there. There was a four-meter hop about an hour ago, but for the most part, their orders seemed random and unfocused. This last move put them closer to Britannica pass, and Hopkins wondered if they were going to risk a direct assault through the valley, a strategy that would only work if they got to move quickly. But after the six-meter hop, the team once again received another set of strange orders from command, asking them to move one meter, then three, then two. *We'll surely be ambushed if we keep dawdling like this*, thought Hopkins.

Much to Hopkins's relief, however, they seemed to be headed towards a small elliptical shaped opening, just a few meters to the right of the valley entrance, and large enough for them to march through single file.

Hopkins was asked to take point. He stepped into the cave, followed by the rest of the battalion. Smiley and the Captain brought up the rear, which didn't seem very leaderly to Hopkins, but made sense since neither one of them thought to bring a weapon to the war. Headquarters radioed in again and instructed them to follow the cave until they could see an exit. This took longer than Hopkins expected because, as before, their orders had them moving random short distances, but eventually he could see the light at the end of the tunnel.

Hopkins studied the cave and ran his hand down the rippled face of the wall. There were hundreds of straight tightly stacked horizontal lines carved into the perfectly concave wall, running the entire length of the tunnel. The tunnel itself was also a perfect straight line from beginning to end, and Hopkins surmised it was man-made. *But why build this secret tunnel and then leave it unguarded?*

Being so close to the exit, Hopkins braved a look, and then quickly ducked back inside when he saw an enemy battalion. Hopkins signalled for everyone to be quiet. Captain Harris squeezed his way past the troops to talk to Hopkins.

"What have we got, Private?"

"Sir, a full enemy battalion, sir," whispered Hopkins.

"Did you see what they were doing? Do you think they know we're here?"

"Sir, I don't think so, sir. They just seem to be standing around. Their captain wasn't looking in this direction, sir."

"Excellent. Looks like we have the element of surprise for once. Get ready."

"You're not leading the push? Sir."

"Are you high, private? I don't have a gun! I was just given these binoculars and told to look for the enemy. Now that we've found them, it's up to you and the rest of the men."

Hopkins couldn't help it; he frowned at his commanding officer.

"Look," said Harris. "I don't make the rules here; I just do what I'm told like you. Base command moves in mysterious ways, and we're just meant to have faith in their grand plan. That plan right now involves me being at the back of this line with Corporal Smiley, while the rest of you get the jump on that battalion out there. Understood, soldier?"

Hopkins nodded, and saluted, and Captain Harris quickly scampered back to join Smiley. Hopkins readied his gun, and signalled the rest of the team to do the same. The order came through, and Smiley tapped the shoulder of the nearest trooper, who in turn tapped the shoulder of the man in front of him, and so on, until Hopkins was tapped, and the men ran out of the cave screaming, "Tally-Bally-Ho!"

Hopkins and the men got the drop on the enemy battalion, and quickly wounded several enemy soldiers as they scrambled to take cover. As the battle raged, Hopkins sensed victory would be theirs, despite a couple of scary moments when the enemy managed to rally and land a few good shots. In the end though, the opposing troops just couldn't recover from the surprise attack, and after a few short minutes, they were all dead.

Silence fell.

The job was done and the victors were selected. The bodies of the enemy soldiers disappeared, along with the cave and the entire valley. Hopkins looked around but couldn't see his team anymore, and he suddenly realized he was standing on a large poster-sized piece of paper with several numbers written on it. Starting at twenty, then eighteen, twelve, eleven, eight, five, all crossed out, ending with the number three. Hopkins's lucky number. He wondered what it all meant, feeling very exposed as he stood alone on the now featureless flat field. Should he head back? Where was "back" anymore? Hopkins heard a voice in the sky. "Alex, you left one of your men on the carpet." And then another voice replied, "Oh, sorry Ian."

Hopkins felt light as a feather, but he'd been here before. The war was over, for now, and he was re-joining his brothers.

There was darkness and peace, again.

3

Rossolington's New Bully

"Time for you and your friend to get to school," said Ian's dad, Tom, the older model clone of Ian; both were tallish, slim, and had short black hair that, from a distance, looked like a swim cap.

Ian opened his bedroom door and handed his dad a piece of a paper.

"What's this?"

"Permission slip. The school is going on a field trip to the pit today."

Clearly irritated, Ian's dad quickly scanned the school document. "And why, may I ask, did you wait until the last minute to show me this?"

"Well," said Ian, "since neither one of us wants me to spend the rest of my life digging for coal, I figured this wouldn't be a big deal. I can either go on the field trip, or spend the afternoon at home with you."

Ian held out a pen, which his dad eagerly used to sign the form.

"Enjoy," said Ian's dad sarcastically. "How about you, umm?"

"Alex," sighed Ian.

"Yes, Alex, sorry. Do you plan to spend all your working life digging like a mole to exploit a limited resource and pollute the planet?"

"No, Mr. Harris. I plan on being a superhero!" Alex stood with his fists pressed against his hips, and his chin held high in the air. Ian's dad was not amused. "Very amusing," he said dryly.

Robin Bank Academy was less than a mile away; a quick walk to the end of York Street and a right turn onto Oxford Street leading to Alexandra Road. A seven-minute walk—usually.

"Yoo-hoo," said Mrs. Pratchett.

It was too late for Alex and Ian to cross the street. Rossolington's big time busybody and organizer for the village's entry into the "Bonny Village" competition walked towards them holding her clipboard.

"Hi, Mrs. Pratchett," said Ian.

"Well hello boys. Going to school?"

Stupid question, thought Ian. "Yes, Mrs. Pratchett."

"Lovely. Listen boys, as you know, every year Rossolington is entered for the South Yorkshire Bonny Village award, and so far I've managed to win it five years in a row!"

Alex and Ian stared blankly at Mrs. Pratchett.

"Yes, Mrs. Pratchett," said Ian.

The plump, brightly dressed lady continued. "Well, I've been doing my rounds, and I've noticed a tiny item that needs addressing."

Mrs. Pratchett's big smile turned upside down and she leaned in closer to Ian. "I know your dad is a busy man, what with all that computer crap he does, but would it kill him to cut his lawn?"

The boys looked back at Ian's front yard. It had become its own eco system, a haven for bugs of all species.

"The Bonny Village judges will be here in a couple of weeks and this yard is letting down York Street. If we can't get this sorted we'll have to make arrangements," said Mrs. Pratchett.

Alex and Ian knew exactly what she meant. Over the years, the Rossolington borough council, with Mrs. Pratchett's permission, had set up a network of people willing to provide obstructions to shield the "Bonny" judges from anything they deemed unworthy. If York Street was indeed marked as unfit for the show, a call would be made to the Mr. Whippy ice cream man or the fire brigade. They would then park themselves at either end of the street and force the judge's car back towards the village's best bits.

"Can you talk to your father?" asked Mrs. Pratchett.

"Yes, Mrs. Pratchett," said Ian.

"Oh good. That's wonderful. I'll swing by tomorrow to see your beautiful yard. Now you children run along. You don't want to be late for school." And with that, Mrs. Pratchett refocused on her clipboard and pushed by the two boys to continue her inspection.

Once she was out of earshot, Alex turned to Ian. "You going to tell your dad to mow the lawn?"

"No. I like ice cream."

Oxford street was next, home to Rossolington's newest bully, Darren Wilkins. He would sit by his bedroom window scanning the street below for his next victim.

The boys kept a watchful eye on Darren's house, and as they walked by, they saw his curtains move. Soon after that his front door opened and, for a moment, they heard what must have been Darren's father yelling something about cigarettes. By the time the door slammed shut, Alex and Ian were almost at the end of the street. The boys, however, were not particularly athletic and their "running" looked more like a distracted power-walk, certainly no match for Darren.

"Hello, boys!" Darren slapped a meaty paw on each of their shoulders, stopping them dead in their tracks. They slowly turned to face him.

Darren was the same age, but had developed freakishly early. He stood almost a foot taller than his two victims and had clearly fallen in love with lifting weights. He didn't look twelve years old either, and hardly ever wore his school uniform, which probably explained why he always managed to smell of cigarettes.

"In a hurry?" Darren asked.

The boys exchanged a glance, but neither had anything to say.

"Forget something, Alex?"

Alex and Ian started to shudder as the fear and anger-inspired adrenaline coursed through their bodies. A horrible cocktail triggering a fight-or-flight response, which also made them incapable of doing either. It cancelled out any thought of using their superior numbers to overpower Darren.

"For a little geeky runt, you're not too bright, are you?"

Darren grabbed one of each boy's ears and pressed his thumbnails against the cartilage inside. Alex and Ian winced and involuntarily tilted their heads away from Darren's fists in a futile attempt to minimize the pain.

"You owe me two weeks' pocket money, and that's about twenty quid, if I've done my math right," said Darren.

He hadn't, but Alex wasn't about to correct him. It was odd that Darren had recently switched to stealing the boys' money. In the past their lunches and snacks were enough to satisfy him. Rossolington's newest bully had stepped up his game, it seemed, and cash was now definitely king. Alex might have thought on that some more, but he was more concerned about the pain in his ear and the mark it might leave. He felt it was time to use the only card he had in his pathetic deck.

"Listen, Darren," said Alex.

Darren pressed harder against their ears.

"Listen. I remember now; we owe you money."

"We?" exclaimed Ian.

"We," said Alex, "owe you money. But if I go home with a mark, my dad—the safety bloke at the pit and someone your dad needs to keep the pit open—is going to ask questions."

Darren's grip loosened slightly. A school bullying problem was hardly cause for the pit to close, but Alex suspected Darren wasn't smart enough to realize that.

"So what do you think is going to happen?" asked Alex.

Thinking for Darren wasn't easy, and his eyes darted left and right as he thought about what Alex had said.

"I know what will happen to you if my dad loses his job," said Darren.

"Yes, I get that. It would be bad," said Alex. "So it seems we should be able to make a deal. Right?"

Darren's grip loosened a little more, as he tried to figure out what that deal would be. Alex made the mistake of rolling his eyes, which pissed Darren off and the ear torture resumed.

"Arrgh, we, and I do mean we," Alex glared at Ian again, "will get you the twenty pounds as long as you agree not to do any damage my dad will notice."

Darren seemed to get it now and he let go of their bright red ears. Alex and Ian furiously rubbed them and repeatedly checked for blood.

"Gotcha, but I want that twenty by the end of the day," said Darren.

Alex and Ian took a step backwards away from Darren.

"We can't do that," said Alex.

Darren stepped forward and reached out to grab their ears again, but the two boys took another step away. "I mean we can't today because we're taking a field trip to the pit this afternoon and my dad will be driving us home afterward. We won't be able to meet you."

"Tomorrow morning then, before school," said Darren.

"Okay," said Alex. "Tomorrow morning. Meet us at the end of York Street near the entrance to the woods."

Darren looked over his shoulder at the meeting point, seeming satisfied with the arrangement. He then playfully smacked Ian around the head to once again show them who was boss before crossing the street. Ian and Alex resumed their walk to school.

"Nice one mate," complained Ian as he rubbed the spot Darren had smacked. "How do you think we're going to get twenty quid by tomorrow morning?"

"I have no idea, but this beats having my ears ripped off."

"And what's going to happen tomorrow when we don't pay up?"

"I don't know. Maybe we can set off earlier and take a longer way to school."

"Get up earlier?" asked Ian, clearly not into the idea of less sleep and more exercise.

"Do you have any better ideas?" asked Alex.

"Not at the moment, but how long do you think we can avoid Darren? He's going to come to school eventually and he'll be looking for us."

The Correct Ratio

Frank pulled into his parking space at the Rossolington Colliery. A sign reserved the spot with the title "Geotech Engineer," and it was clearly subjected to frequent deliberate abuse. The "tech" part of the title had also been crossed out and replaced with "idiot." That was new, but not the worst thing he'd been called at the mine.

Being the resident stick-in-the-mud and person in charge of safety was not a position that made Frank many friends. His actions would often hurt the mine's cash flow, and subsequently everyone's bank balance.

The Rossolington Colliery was huge. The initial estimates on the amount of coal underneath the little village made the mine one of the largest in the world, and the most profitable too. Being the person who could stop production in order to maintain the pit's perfect safety record, made Frank public enemy number one to the mine's owners, and a major thorn in the side of Mr. Donald Brock, the man who kept raising quotas, and (as Frank suspected) lining his own pockets.

Frank's less than lofty standing at the company also meant his office wasn't really an office at all, just a simple desk at the end of a corridor next to a small filing cabinet. Government regulations guaranteed his position at the mine, but not the quality of his work area. His desk was also positioned across the hall from the men's toilet, and no amount of Sharon's potpourri was going to mask the smell that came from there. Frank would frequently return to his desk to find the door deliberately wedged open so he could truly appreciate the symphony of odours emanating from within.

"Morning, Frank!"

Frank turned from his computer to greet Mike Ridley, the mine's lead crew supervisor, a middle-aged burly teddy bear of a man seemingly designed around his big bright smile. Mike, dressed in a bright orange safety vest, stood over six feet tall and was almost as wide as the corridor leading to Frank's "office."

"Morning," said Frank. "Did you see my parking sign this morning?"

"Yeah, I just saw that earlier. I'll get someone to clean it up before the kids arrive. I wouldn't worry about it. Deep down the lads do appreciate what you do here."

"You could have fooled me."

Frank locked his computer and grabbed his jacket, lunch tin, and hardhat.

"Is that new seam ready for inspection?" asked Frank.

"Yes, they've got the first couple of rooms dug out. I just don't think you're going to like it."

"Really? Why?"

Mike gestured for Frank to follow him. "You'll see."

Frank and Mike made their way through the office and then outside towards the main shaft building and the cage that would take them down into the mine. Mondays at the pit were usually a little quieter while everyone slowly shrugged off the weekend's hangovers. But today they were entertaining visitors from all the local schools, so Frank wasn't surprised to find everyone busily trying to clear pathways and clean windows. There seemed to be a lot fewer calendars[1] on the walls too.

Before being allowed down into the mine, Frank had instituted several extra safety procedures. The first involved the installation of highly sensitive smoke detectors in the corridor leading to the cage room because, amazingly, one or two miners would always forget to finish their cigarettes before heading down into a cave made of fuel and filled with all manner of flammable gases. The second procedure involved a mandatory breathalyser test that unlocked the turnstiles and let the miners into the office to pick up their safety equipment. It was a simple, inexpensive setup that met surprising resistance before it was installed. An alarming number of miners it seemed thought it was perfectly okay to arrive at work drunk, and then operate heavy machinery in one of the most dangerous places on the planet. Frank couldn't wrap his head around the thinking of these people sometimes and often wondered if they'd dowse themselves in petrol and light a match if the paycheque was decent enough.

Once Frank and Mike cleared the turnstiles, they made their way to the equipment room where Gladice, the octogenarian and longest serving employee at the colliery, greeted them with a forced smile. "Frank, Mike."

"Good morning, Gladice. How are you today?" asked Frank.

Gladice ignored the question, slowly stood up, and walked to the large storage units installed behind her desk. She opened a compartment, pulled out two bright yellow bags, and dumped them on her desk in front of Frank and Mike.

---

[1] The inspirational kind loaded with pictures of beautiful motorcycles and cars, apparently operated by women who don't mind the cold.

"Okay." Gladice sighed as she carefully sat down again, picked up a clipboard from her desk, and loaded it with the correct checklist. Frank and Mike opened their bags and started to assemble the safety equipment on Gladice's desk.

"One working torch?" asked Gladice.

The men picked up their torches and turned them on and off again several times. Frank also tested the light on his hardhat by shining it in Mike's face. Mike fired back. Gladice sighed.

"One working whistle?" The resulting whistle-off made Gladice roll her eyes.

"One breathing kit, fully charged?"

Mike and Frank checked the small metal tank in their kit. A pressure gauge at the top confirmed their air tanks were full. Gladice checked another box on her form, turned her clipboard towards the two men, and pointed to where she needed them to sign.

With their equipment checked, Mike and Frank entered the cage. Mike closed the gate and hit a large red button to start the long descent into the mine. Very quickly, daylight was replaced by a blueish glow from the hodgepodge of fluorescent lamps as they passed each level in the mine. Frank studied the spaces between each floor as they continued down. "Is it me, or are these layers of roof rock getting thinner?"

"It's you. They're within guidelines."

Frank nodded but wasn't happy.

"Have we broken the record yet?" ask Frank.

"Yup, we're past 1,600 meters. Excited?"

Frank had known Mike for a while now and considered him a trusted ally at the pit. He knew when his friend was being sarcastic.

"Oh, I'm over the moon. I can't wait to hear that moron Brock applaud himself at the next company Christmas doo when he talks about *his* record breaking mine."

Mike looked wistful. "Ah yes, drinking watered-down cider from those little plastic champagne glasses, eating those rank sausage rolls his wife makes. That Brock knows how to throw a party that's for sure."

The elevator reached the base of the mine, and the two men let themselves out. At this level, this deep, the mine felt like the loneliest place on Earth. The black walls seemed to swallow the light coming from their headlamps. The seam crackled and popped as the weight of over 1,600 meters of rock and dirt pressed down on the new rooms dug out of the coal. At this level, at these pressures, the walls were like radiators and the two men immediately started to sweat, causing the fine coal powder in the air to stick to their faces.

"I've been doing this for over ten years," said Mike, "and I've never liked that sound."

"You shouldn't. I think the pit's telling us we've gone too far."

The two men walked into the nearest room, past the first pillar into a second room where they found the Constant Miner, powered down, lying dormant like a hibernating beast waiting for winter to end. Its massive sixteen foot cutting drum was now temporarily satisfied after chewing on the coal to create the first rooms in the new seam. Frank turned his headlamp back towards the first pillar.

"I didn't think it would take you long to notice," said Mike.

Frank walked around the pillar between the two rooms, shining his light along the surface of the coal wall.

"This isn't wide enough," sighed Frank.

Mike looked down at the ground and shook his head.

"Does that idiot Brock think he can change the ratio? 60:40, it's supposed to be 60:40. This deep, there's a good argument for 50:50."

Mike shrugged.

"Come on, Mike. You know this is dangerous. We take out sixty percent, and make supporting pillars out of the rest. That's the rule! What is this? Sixty-five? Seventy?"

"I know, but—"

"But nothing Mike. What? Did Brock increase the quota again?"

"We get a bonus if we beat this one too."

Frank shook his head and sighed. "Sorry Mike, you won't be getting that bonus. I'm not letting anyone work in here until we've brought down some supports for these rooms, and then the rest of the seam can be dug at 50:50 or I'm shutting this mine down."

Frank propped his lunch tin against the pillar wall and continued his inspection.

C H A P T E R

Nanobots

The nanobot was as old as the coal that had held it captive, but it had just rebuilt itself new that morning. The micrometre[2] sized insectoid robot was now free to crawl and explore after spending millions of years trapped underneath tons of fossilized vegetation.

It was aware of two large lifeforms nearby, but its chemical hail was being ignored. It also detected a small object placed just millimetres away. This was new and not native to this environment, clearly something constructed to fulfil a purpose, and was possibly transported here by the nearby lifeforms. The nanobot speculated they were also responsible for creating the new opening around them, which set the minuscule robot free, and caused its reboot rebuild cycle.

The nanobot attempted to communicate with the nearby object, but again, received no answer to its chemical hail. It then scanned the object and discovered it was metallic, hollow,

---

[2] One micron is equal to one millionth of a meter. These tiny machines could use a single strand of spider silk for a hammock.

and seemingly inert, designed to protect something held within its crudely finished outer shell.

The nanobot re-calibrated its sensors to adjust for the crude metal, and after a second scan, detected organic matter inside the container. There were three objects: one dead and two others that seemed to be some form of plant life, slowly dying after being detached from their source of nourishment, possibly containing seeds to pass along its genetic code and grow anew.

The dead object was more interesting.

It was constructed from several ingredients with a highly complex centre section composed of a set of manufactured chemicals mixed with plant material. Surrounded by flat plates made of another set of components designed to hold the centre section captive. These softer plates also contained plant material but were long dead after apparently being exposed to intense heat for an unknown amount of time.

The nanobot signalled the others, who booted up, wirelessly connected to their companion, and within a microsecond knew everything that had been discovered so far about the vessel and its contents. As a collective, they decided to investigate further.

Several million nanobots reached the container and surveyed it. Its height, weight and composition were quickly studied and logged. Its construction seemed simplistic, but effective enough to protect the organic matter inside from the many incompatible elements in the immediate vicinity. There was, however, a weakness in the object's construction in that it seemed to be made of two separate pieces latched together. The collective analysed the small gap between the separate sections and calculated it was easily wide enough to let the nanobots inside to investigate further.

Once inside, the collective split up into three groups and targeted each one of the organic objects. And though each group was now operating independently, they kept communications open over their local wireless network to share information.

What followed was a detailed breakdown of the objects down to the cellular level. Proteins, sugars, fibres, fats, acids and minerals. These objects represented a long lineage and had also been coated with a set of complex chemicals, which the group's collective intelligence surmised must be a backup defence if the larger metallic container was not available. And though they couldn't express it, the manner in which all this information flew back and forth suggested the nanobots were happy to be studying something new.

Within milliseconds they had a complete understanding of each object, knew how to improve them and delay the deterioration of the still living plant based components. They surmised the objects in the container were probably constructed and assembled by the lifeforms they had detected earlier, possibly to be consumed as fuel. A millisecond later a plan was agreed upon and the self-replication process began.

Their long incarceration was finally at an end, and they would be able to complete their mission.

CHAPTER 6

The Eat in Nine Bites Method

As the mini-bus hauled twelve less than enthused Robin Bank pupils into the Rossolington colliery car park, Alex saw his dad impatiently staring at his watch. They were two minutes late. Their actual tour of the mine wouldn't start for another half an hour, but Alex knew how his dad was. Late was late.

This could be a long afternoon, thought Alex. If he could just get through this without his dad acknowledging any family connection, he might almost enjoy this break away from school. The bus doors swung open, and everyone lazily dragged themselves outside.

"Son?"

Urgh!

At first Alex pretended he didn't hear anything, simultaneously hoping the ground would swallow him whole. Since the parking lot cement seemed stubbornly set on remaining intact, he lifted his head and shyly waved.

Alex's dad looked him directly in the eye. "Perhaps you'd like to tell the group how long the Rossolington mine has been in operation."

Alex glared back at his father. He had to know that singling him out from the group like this was incredibly embarrassing.

Why would he acknowledge the family connection? Perhaps his father took some pleasure from torturing him with this surprise quiz.

"Err, the pit was sunk between 1912 and 1914," said Alex.

"Incorrect, 1912 and 1915."

Alex looked over at Ian and caught him smiling.

"Between 1912 and 1915 the pit was sunk, and you are standing on one of the largest deposits of coal in the world. Does anyone know how deep the mine goes? Alex?"

Really? Again with the quiz time. "1,400 meters?"

"Incorrect, again. As of this week, the mine is now just a little over 1,600 meters deep, which is officially a world record for a coal mine."

Really? Asking him a question he couldn't possibly know the answer to. A new record-breaking low had also been achieved in their relationship. Alex glanced around at the other kids, as they smiled and avoided eye contact with him.

Alex's father continued. "My name is Mr. Adams, and after the rest of the buses arrive and we've all had some lunch, I'll be taking you on a tour. Until then we'll need you to wait in the breakroom. Just head into the large building in front of you and take a left. My son Alex here knows the way."

Alex cringed at being deputized as daddy's official helper. But getting away from this attention seemed like a good idea, so he wasted no time leading the small group to the break room. Once inside, Alex was free to explore the old vending machine in the corner of the room and use his pocket money to purchase something hopefully still within its eat-by-date.

"What do you think you're doing?" asked Ian.

"Getting something to eat," said Alex.

"Oh yeah? With what money?"

"I've got three pound, why?"

"Remember this morning? Darren? He's going to beat us up tomorrow if we don't give him twenty quid."

"Yeah, but three pound isn't twenty, and I'm hungry."

"That's true, it's not twenty, but with the four quid I have that only leaves us with thirteen to find before tomorrow morning."

Alex turned towards the vending machine and stared longingly at his target. Two slightly mangled Lion bars[3] were perched awkwardly at the front of their column in the machine. He wondered if, given the right nudge, it might be convinced to deliver both bars for the price of one. "But what are we going to have for lunch?"

"Nothing, I guess."

"Nothing?" Alex's stomach angrily growled at Ian. "Do you hear that? I'm starving."

"I know, so am I." Ian pulled Alex away from the vending machine and sat him down at a nearby table, facing away from his prize.

"Think of it this way," said Ian, "we now have seven pounds. I think I have a couple more in my piggy bank at home. You might too."

Alex shook his head.

"Okay, maybe not, but in any case, we might already be half-way to not having our ears ripped off tomorrow. Could you ask your dad for some money?"

Alex shook his head again. "But my mum might give me five if I say it's for a school project."

"Great. I think I can get five from my dad. I'll tell him it's for a book."

---

[3] Wafer, caramel, and crisp cereal covered in milk chocolate. No Lions are harmed during the production of this piece of confectionery.

"Brilliant, but in order for this plan to work we have to go hungry."

"Well, it's either that or ear torture," said Ian.

Suddenly, a lunch tin was placed on the table in front of the two boys.

"You kids hungry?" asked Alex's dad as he opened the container.

Alex looked inside the tin and saw two of the largest and juiciest apples he had ever seen sitting on top of a thick well-stuffed peanut butter sandwich. Alex lunged for the sandwich.

"Not so fast," said Alex's dad, and he slapped Alex's hand away. "Where are your manners?" Alex's dad reached inside and grabbed both apples, taking one for himself, and offered the other to the two boys.

"Ian will take the apple, he doesn't like peanuts," said Alex.

"Okay, then," said Alex's dad, and he handed the apple to Ian. "I'll see you kids after lunch."

Frank walked away from the boys and joined Mike who had been patiently waiting for his lunch buddy outside the breakroom.

"What's the apple for?" asked Mike.

"I don't know actually. It looked really good."

"Do you really want to spoil your appetite? Waste valuable stomach space on that apple?"

Frank looked at the apple again and mentally replayed the conversation he had had with Sharon after breakfast. He wasn't sure what struck him about it because he'd seen and ignored plenty of apples before. Mike, on the other hand, did make a good point about stomach space, and a sumptuous beer-battered burger and gravy-covered chips awaited. The apple ended up in the closest rubbish bin.

Ian and Alex were enjoying their good fortune. Not only had they scored a free lunch, but they had also managed to get the best tasting apple and most delicious peanut butter sandwich ever assembled.

"I've had apples before," said Ian, "but this is amazing. You want to try a bite?"

"Are you kidding? This sandwich is fantastic. It's peanut butter, which I love, but somehow better. I wonder if my mum added something."

The two boys continued eating in silence, taking their time between bites to savour the flavours hoping to prolong the experience for as long as possible. Ian carefully turned the apple around in his hand between bites to properly select the next best part of the fruit to enjoy. Alex held his sandwich in both hands as he methodically applied his "eat in nine bites" plan, mentally separating the sandwich into three rows, which would require three bites each, figuring each bite would not be a paltry nibble, or too big to comfortably enjoy.

Alex took his sandwich eating very seriously.

7

Pick Your Prize

Donald Brock, the chief executive in charge of operations at the Rossolington colliery, lovingly eyed five small towers of twenty pound notes on his expensive desk. Each tower was twice as large as the stack to its left and about an inch apart, making the last pile four thousand pounds tall.

Donald leaned closer to the money, smelt it and smiled. He sat back in his Nappa leather chair, which creaked and groaned a little as his short, portly frame pushed against the plush well-padded piece of furniture.

A small red light began to flash on his desk phone, and Donald positioned his wire frame glasses further down his round nose to see who was calling. The call was from his latest secretary, Natalie. "Yes?"

"Mike Ridley to see you, Mr. Brock."

"Oh good. Umm, is he clean?"

There was a deliberate pause as Natalie formulated an answer to that question.

"Yes, Mr. Brock, he's a big clean teddy bear."

"Err, thank you, Natalie," said Donald, a little taken aback by his new secretary's candid nature. Donald wondered where

31

his wife found this one. She was the third secretary he'd had in the last year and would likely last as long as the others once that bubbly, down to earth personality collided with his wife's paranoia. Donald had to remember to never compliment the help, especially in front of the wife. "Could you send him in, please?"

Across the office from Donald's desk, a set of heavy double doors opened, and Natalie, a spectacular mass of gravity-defying blonde hair attached to a toy troll-like body, led Mike into the room. Donald rolled his eyes as Natalie ogled the large burly miner.

"Here you are Mr. Brock, Mike Ridley."

Donald jumped up excitedly, and walked toward Mike with his arm outstretched. "Mike! Nice to see you again. Thank you Natalie."

Donald took and vigorously shook Mike's hand. Natalie slowly backed up through the double doors, and closed them.

"She new?" asked Mike.

"Umm, yes, she started last week. My wife hired her. Doing okay, I guess. She certainly seemed to like you."

"You reckon?" Mike looked back at the doors.

"Are you kidding me? Big strapping lad like you, I'm sure you're beating them off with a stick."

"Not really Mr. Brock. My wife broke that stick into lots of little pieces five years ago."

Donald winced and wished he was better at socializing with the commoners.

"Umm, right, you're married to, err?"

"Samantha."

"Right, Samantha."

Donald had no clue who Samantha was, but pictured a stout woman wearing an apron, menacingly beating the palm of her hand with a rolling pin. He scanned his memory for any clarifying images, anything with his mind's creation of Samantha standing next to the man currently in his office. He got nothing. "Well, anyway, sausage roll?"

Donald reached for a small plastic container on his desk and pried open the lid. "My wife made them."

Mike looked inside the container. There they were, the infamous and only offering from the Brock family kitchen and the saddest looking sausage rolls known to miner. A cross between a toad in the hole[4] and an angry pizza.

Mike looked pained. "No, thank you, Mr. Brock, I just had lunch."

"Ha! I don't blame you!" Donald put the lid back on the container. "They're pretty bad if I'm honest. I don't know how my wife does it. She doesn't even make the filling or pastry; she buys all that. All she does is roll one with the other but still can't make a decent sausage roll."

Donald walked over to his window overlooking the main office floor. Mike slowly followed and Donald caught him eyeing up the cash on his desk.

"How's the school tour going?" asked Donald as he watched Frank lead another group of bored kids through the office below them.

"Okay, I guess."

"Don't they enjoy these visits?"

"I expect most of these kids think they're going to leave Rossolington and explore the world."

"That's nice. You know what I see?"

"What's that, Mr. Brock?"

---

4   Toads as in sausage, and sausage as in made of pork. No toads are harmed during the production of this English delicacy. This dish continues the long British tradition of giving unpalatable names to food. Spotted Dick isn't - it just isn't!

"Future employees. Sure, some of them will actually study and find careers elsewhere. But with most of them, we've planted the seed. That's why I get the school to organize these trips. The next time they're not enjoying maths or physics, they'll think, I've got a guaranteed job with a liveable wage waiting for me at the mine. That's regular money and security, and all I have to do is dig coal."

Donald turned and walked back to his desk.

"Do you see these piles of cash on my desk, Mike?"

"Yes, Mr. Brock."

Donald sat down in his chair and shuffled forward to be closer to the money. He pointed at the largest pile. "In two weeks, if we reach our quota from that new seam, this pile of cash, this nice large pile of cash—is your bonus."

Donald enjoyed watching Mike's eyes bulge.

"Does your wife Samantha like to go on holiday, Mike?"

"Oh yes, Mr. Brock, our bloody kitchen table is always covered with brochures. It's all she ever talks about."

"Great," said Donald. "This nice big pile here. That's easily two weeks in the South of France. Beautiful part of the world. Relaxing. You and your wife will have the vacation of a lifetime down there. If we meet our quota in time."

Mike winced.

"This next pile of cash is your bonus if we're a couple of days late meeting that quota. Not bad. Probably a week in Ibiza. A little sun and sand, maybe some clubbing if that's your thing. It'll be a nice trip."

Donald gave Mike a little time to process the two holiday ideas.

"This third pile, the four days past quota pile," said Donald, eyeing the money like it was covered in mould. "This might be good for a nice weekend in Paris. Not too bad, but only a weekend. No time for you or your wife to explore. Just a quick hop over for some cheap duty-free, weird food, and rude Parisians before heading back. Parlez-vous français?"

"What?"

"Make that very rude. They do like foreigners to make the effort, Mike."

Donald shifted his attention to the next pile of cash.

"This one might get you a weekend in a B&B in Blackpool. The bright lights, fish and chips, and donkey rides. Do you think your wife will be happy with a donkey ride on her holiday?"

Donald watched Mike run this new scenario through his head. Judging by the facial acrobatics Mike was making, the pitch wasn't going well. "Probably not."

"Understandable, really. We've gone all the way from two luxurious weeks in the South of France to this, the last pile. The two weeks over quota pile. A night on the town right here in good old Rossolington. A few hours in the pub and maybe a curry on the way home. Would your wife like that instead of a holiday?"

"Err no, Mr. Brock, she most certainly wouldn't."

Donald stood up and pointed at the cash again, one pile at a time. "South of France, week in Ibiza, weekend in Paris, Blackpool, night out in Rosso. It's up to you Mike, you're the lead crew supervisor. We've got a couple of weeks to meet that quota and, as I understand it, our resident government stooge just shut down the new seam."

"Err, well, yes sir, he did, but—"

Donald raised his hand for Mike to stop speaking. "It's up to you, Mike. It can be you and the missus in the South of France for a dream vacation, or a night throwing up curry at home."

CHAPTER

Pins and Needles

Alex, Graham, Ian, and Robert waited in the breakroom to be picked up. All the other kids got to take the buses home, but they had been told to wait. At 5pm, Alex's dad strolled into the room. "Let's go, chop chop, what are you waiting for?"

Alex nudged Robert to wake him up and the kids slowly flopped out of their chairs and dragged themselves outside.

Alex turned to Ian. "How do you feel?"

"Why?"

"Not sure, I've just felt weird all afternoon. Like pins and needles all over, but a little different. Like really tiny ants crawling under my skin. You know what I mean?"

"I do, actually."

"You do?"

"Yeah, it started right after lunch. My stomach hurt a little at first, but after that, pins and needles in my arms and legs, everywhere, inside and out."

"Weird. I thought it might be that sandwich, but you ate the apple," said Alex.

"I know. Coal dust maybe? Is this what black lung feels like?"

"I doubt it. It's not like we spent a long time down there during the tour. Plus, my dad's the safety bloke so I don't think he'd let us go if it were dangerous."

The group walked up to Frank's car in the parking lot and piled in. Alex, being the second most senior Adams, nabbed the front passenger seat.

Before they turned into York Street, Frank pulled the car over to the curb and stopped. Robert, Graham, Ian, and Alex exchanged a glance, and then Frank turned to Alex. "Do you want to drive the car home?"

"Ay?" said everyone except Frank.

"Do you want to drive the car home, Alex?"

Alex had to let this sink in a little. He was pretty certain his father had just offered to let him drive the car onto York street, and then take it the rest of the way home. A journey less than half a mile, but to Alex it may as well have been to China. This was all parts fantastic and scary at the same stupendous time. Suddenly, the car seemed massive.

"But I can't reach the pedals."

"Like you'd even know what to do with them." Frank laughed. "You just sit on my lap and steer, and I'll work the gears."

Alex excitedly passed his school bag and his father's lunch tin to Ian, noting the wide-eyed expressions of envy and fear the back seat crew were giving him. He then shifted himself over to his dad's lap and put his hands on the steering wheel. Alex gave it an experimental turn left and right; it felt heavy and hard to move. He looked down at his feet, only an inch away from the pedals but close enough to rest comfortably on his father's work boots.

Frank pressed his big left foot down on the clutch and his left hand put the car in first gear. Alex was suddenly aware of everything in the car; he could hear what must be the gears shifting underneath him. He tightened his grip on the steering wheel.

"Okay," said Frank, "we're in first gear. I'm going to take off slowly and I want you to listen. When I say turn left, start to turn the wheel. Just follow my instructions, okay?"

Alex nodded.

Frank looked over his shoulder to make sure there wasn't any traffic, and then slowly lifted his foot off the clutch and gently pressed on the accelerator. The car started to creep forward and Alex felt the steering get lighter.

"Okay, start your turn," said Frank.

Alex slowly turned the wheel and the car veered left. He had seen his dad drive many times before, but it now seemed weird that this small wheel could control such a huge machine. Alex enjoyed the power he felt but was suddenly distracted by a pins and needles sensation in his feet. First in the left foot and then in the right.

"A little quicker son."

"Ay? Oh!" Alex turned the wheel a little faster and the car turned into York Street. The turn ended up being a little wide, but still within the correct lane. He could hear Graham exhale behind him. Frank switched to second gear and the car started to speed up. Alex couldn't recall a time when he had concentrated so hard. The car was only doing ten miles an hour, but it felt like light speed. The pins and needles sensation started to travel up his legs. The left leg followed by the right leg, weirdly to a steady rhythm. Left, right, left, right, tick, tock, tick, tock. Shins, calves, shins, calves, left knee, right knee.

"Now, up ahead you're going to follow the road to the right, but you need to take a wide arc, so turn a little to the left first. Okay?"

"Okay," said Alex.

The section of York Street they were on became much wider before it turned right, and Alex could see what he had to do. He slowly turned left to get closer to the curb. This would give any oncoming traffic turning into their section of the street plenty of room.

Alex tried to concentrate, but the pins and needles had now moved up to his thighs. As his heart beat faster, it seemed to get worse and the sensation leapt to his groin before moving up to his belly, chest, arms and then his fingers. He tightened his grip on the wheel and tried to refocus. He wanted to enjoy this moment. Frank put the car into third gear and the car surged up to twenty miles an hour. Alex took a deep breath and the prickly sensation climbed up his neck and tickled his ears.

"Okay, start to make a wide arc to the right."

"What?" asked Alex, distracted by the faint rustling sound inside his ears.

"Turn right. Now."

Alex turned the wheel clockwise, pulling with his right hand, and pushing with the left. Text book, if a little late, and the car's tires squealed as they struggled to grip the road and make the turn.

"A little quicker son."

Out of the corner of his eye, Alex could see his father's right hand creeping upward towards the steering wheel. Just in case. So Alex refocused and made sure he pointed the car towards the correct side of the street and finished the turn. The hand was lowered again, and the car was put into fourth gear. Thirty miles an hour. Alex took a deep breath and tried to focus on the road ahead. The parked cars on either side of the street were flying by so quickly now. This was warp speed, and he was captain of the ship. Part of him wanted to drive all day, but he was also a little relieved to see his house fast approaching on the left. He was tense yet excited, nervous but the most awake he'd ever been in his life. The pins and needles had finally stopped too.

Alex's dad gently pushed his foot on the break, pressed on the clutch pedal, and then switched down to third gear.

"Okay son, let go of the wheel. Let me park."

Alex was a little disappointed he couldn't finish the trip, but also glad his part of the task was done. It had been a brief, yet epic adventure and a lot to process. As they approached the house, Frank turned towards the curb, put the car in neutral and coasted to a stop. Graham and Robert bolted for their door, quickly exiting the vehicle, and ran into the house. Ian opened the door on his side of the car, but before he left, he patted Alex on the shoulder. "Nice one, mate."

"Nice work, son."

"I did okay?" asked Alex.

"A little slow on your turns, but for your first time behind the wheel, you did great."

Alex was on top of the world, and he heard "first time" to mean, there would be a "second time" or maybe even a "third time" behind the wheel.

"Okay, dinner time," said Frank.

Alex climbed onto the passenger seat and then retrieved his bag and lunch tin.

"Just do me a favour, son."

"What?"

"If your mother asks, tell her I ate my packed lunch today. Okay?"

Alex smiled. "Sure, dad."

C H A P T E R

The Galactic Makeover

It was Tuesday, 6:30am. Alex's dad peed and then farted, Graham and Robert giggled, and Alex's mum complained, "Frank Adams!"

Alex lay sound asleep, and even though his dad's wakeup call sounded like a flock of doves flying into a wood chipper, Alex didn't stir. Even the traditional battle for the bathroom, and Robert's tantrum about not getting to wear mismatched socks could wake him. He was out for the count and lost in a dream.

Alex found himself in a narrow, pristine white room with walls easily one hundred feet tall. There was also no visible way to leave; no doors or windows.

Several thin panels around the room slid open, and long robotic arms appeared carrying an assortment of tools. Similar to robots Alex had seen on television building cars, but sleeker and more graceful, armour-plated with a shiny pearl white finish. Some of them seemed pretty harmless as they advanced clutching a towel or a large bucket, while others were more worrisome as they approached Alex holding a scalpel or a saw.

The last arm to appear carried a large container and placed it on the floor. A label on the lid read: PARTS.

Alex was not worried because he knew this was a dream, and somehow, he knew good things were going to happen. The robots painlessly removed both his arms and placed them in the bucket. New, more muscular ones were pulled out of the parts box and attached without leaving a scar. He did wonder why there was no blood gushing out of his body during this operation, but figured some part of his brain (the part that gets grossed out by the sight of the stuff) must have requested this experience be kid-friendly, so he didn't think too much of it.

Once the arms were done, the machines moved on to his legs. Alex giggled as two robot arms took hold of his torso, while four others, two for each leg, got to work and replaced his limbs with something a world class sprinter would be proud of. They were long, muscular and powerful, but to scale for a twelve-year-old boy. Alex gave each one a twist and flex once they were attached. He really liked the direction this dream was going.

The torso work, on the other hand, he could have done without. First came the probe, a long tube with a sharp tip jabbed into his belly through the button to suck out the fat. It didn't hurt, but the belly wobble and sucking sound were really embarrassing. He also suspected the robot doing the work was deliberately hitting that area harder to punish him, clearly disappointed at the quantity of fat it had to remove. Following that lovely procedure, more probes were employed. Smaller ones, designed to tackle the details around the chest area and torso. Each one pierced the skin and then left only after every muscle was gently shocked into the optimum shape. It even tickled a little, and Alex for the first time realized he was only wearing his Batman underpants.

After the operation was complete, Alex was lowered, his bare feet touching the cold floor. Each robot arm then slid back into the hole it emerged from, and Alex was left alone to admire his new body. *This was nice,* he thought, and he only wished he wasn't dreaming it. Alex then noticed a door was being lowered into the room, settling five feet in front of him. There was a knock, and Alex answered to find his mother waiting on the other side, looking irritated with her arms crossed, impatiently tapping her foot. "Wake up!"

"Yeah but mum, did you see what the robot doctors did?"

"I don't care what the robot doctors did, you're going to be late for school. Wake up!"

Alex's mum put her hand into her dressing gown pocket and pulled out a bright red toy fire engine. She threw it at Alex's head. "WAKE UP!"

Alex awoke with a jolt to find his mother's face six inches away from his.

"Wow, you are out of it this morning. You're going to be late for school so move it!"

"Okay, mum," said Alex, petrified and holding the covers close to his chin.

Once his mother left and slammed the door, Alex pushed back the covers and looked at his body. Two things struck him. The first was the notion that he must still be dreaming because the Olympic-ready physique given to him by his robot surgeons was still there. The second was how clearly he could see everything in his room without his glasses. From his new small scale Mr. Universe body to the Star Trek posters on his walls, everything was in sharp crystal clear high definition.

I must still be dreaming, thought Alex, but he decided to play along until he properly woke up. He didn't want to irritate his dream mum any more than he had to after all. His first stop in the bathroom to brush his teeth gave him another nice surprise. His misaligned, pointy, cavity-filled teeth were gone, and in their place, perfectly straight, pure white gnashers. Alex smiled at himself in the bathroom mirror. He then snarled and growled and made claws with his hands, only to notice the white spots on his fingernails had disappeared too. Alex held them out at arm's length to properly admire them, until it started to feel weird to do so. He compensated by flexing his biceps. *As dreams go, this was going straight in at number one.*

"ALEX!" screamed Sharon. "Ian's here. Bloody hurry up!"

Alex found an old belt to hold up his now very roomy shorts, and an even older white shirt to wear that pre-dated his peanut butter loving belly. He grabbed his school bag and tie and ran downstairs. His goal was to rush out the front door before his mother saw his new body wrapped in old, ill-fitting clothing.

"Wait just a bloody moment young man," commanded Sharon.

Alex stopped dead in his tracks, his shoulders dropping. *Oh well, the dream was fun while it lasted.*

Sharon stepped up to Alex and placed her hand on his forehead[5]. "Are you feeling okay? You've lost weight."

"I actually feel really good, mum," said Alex.

Alex's mother finished her palm scan and grabbed Alex's necktie to construct a simple four-in-hand knot around his neck. "Have you been exercising?"

---

[5] A mother's hand on the forehead. Better than an x-ray, cat scan, MRI and medical tricorder—combined!

"Err, yeah. Been playing bulldog a lot lately," said Alex. Sharon finished his tie and kissed Alex on the forehead. "Well okay then, good boy, be careful."

Sharon was more concerned than she was letting on, and the fact that Alex wasn't wearing his glasses hadn't gone unnoticed either. She weighed the cost of further investigating her son's sudden transformation against her precious quiet time in the house. It wasn't like he had a temperature, after all. Sharon returned to her recliner and picked up her little black note book. She found the page she was working on, crossed out 826 and wrote 827 next to it.

Alex passed Ian waiting outside, grabbed one of the handles on Ian's bag and dragged him into the street.

Ian followed (he didn't have much choice), barely keeping his footing as they both quickly made their way down York Street.

"Hold on mate, I've got to talk to you," said Ian, "I had a wicked dream last night."

Alex stopped dead in his tracks, and took a fresh look at Ian from top to bottom. The first thing he noticed was Ian's acne, because it was gone. "Really? How do you feel this morning?"

"Proper amazing. I had this dream, I was in this—"

"White room?"

"Err, yeah, and these—"

"Robot arms?"

"Err, right! Holy moly, you had the same dream?"

"Maybe. Maybe I'm still dreaming. I don't need my glasses today, my teeth are perfect, and most of my clothes don't fit anymore."

Ian punched Alex in the arm.

"Ow! What did you do that for?"

"Still think you're dreaming?"

"Not sure. I like you less, I can tell you that much."

The two boys continued down York Street.

"Alex. I don't think this is a dream. I think we've been infected by some kind of super special coal dust or something."

Alex wasn't convinced. "Really? Magical coal dust? My dad has worked at the pit for years and nothing like this has ever happened to him."

"Maybe it doesn't work on adults."

"Oh come on!"

"Well do you have any better ideas?"

"What about the lunch we had yesterday? You have to admit, there was something strange about it."

Ian appeared to work this new information into his theory. "Right, ah, so, your dad brought his lunch tin into the mine. It got infected with magical coal dust. We ate it, and now we're super fit!"

"Well maybe. At least your theory is getting better."

"You know what I noticed first?"

"What?" asked Alex.

"The scar those kids gave me that time they threw that glass at my knee. It's gone."

"Really?"

"Yeah, and I've felt super brainy all morning. I got up early, did all my homework in ten minutes. So easy. Even the maths. I can't believe it, I actually enjoyed maths!"

At that moment, Alex's newly sharp mind focused on a single thought.

"Oh no, I forgot about Darren."

"Bollocks, did you ask your mum for the five pounds?" asked Ian.

"No, I forgot. I slept in."

Alex and Ian reached the end of York Street and looked towards their meeting point with Darren. They were relieved to find it didn't have a Darren in it.

"Maybe he forgot?" said Alex.

Suddenly, from behind, the boys' once again felt an ear get clamped by one of Darren's meaty paws. "Not likely, nerds!"

CHAPTER 10

A New Perspective

The funny thing about violence is, it mostly requires *will*. Not strength so much, though that's usually a good place to start. Just the confidence to commit, along with a complete lack of empathy and intelligence. In this regard, Darren seemed well-qualified, and was ready to commit some violence on Alex and Ian.

Alex could feel Darren having to work that much harder to force them into the woods behind York Street, now that both he and Ian were no longer their usual pathetic physical state. Alex, however, couldn't muster the will to test out his new body and put this bully in his place. So he unhappily complied with the ear torture and mentally prepared himself as best he could for a beating.

"You got the twenty?" asked Darren. He let go of their ears and pushed the boys over onto the dirt. "Well?"

"We couldn't get it," said Alex. "We have, err…"

"Fifteen!" shouted Ian, nervously. "We have fifteen." Ian got back onto his feet and pulled the money out of his pocket to give to Darren.

Rossolington's premier league bully, however, wasn't having it, and he punched Ian in the face. The blow sent Ian spinning back to the ground, as he cupped his hands over his nose.

"HEY!" shouted Alex.

"Shut up you! Fifteen quid isn't going to do it; I needed twenty. Ian's dad doesn't work at the pit so I can do whatever I like to him." And to prove his point, he gave Ian's rib cage a swift kick with his steel toe-capped boots. Ian cried out in pain and pulled his knees up to protect his chest. Alex could have sworn he heard a bone crack and felt a chill wash over him. Darren had never been this bad before; this fight was getting out of control. Their little world seemed to pause for a moment, and ever so briefly, Darren didn't seem as confident.

Alex, seeing his friend on the floor in pain and realizing the entire reason they didn't have all the cash was his fault, boiled over with rage and guilt. He quickly scrambled to his feet and took a swing at Darren. Being that this was the first time he'd taken a swing at anything, however, he found that Darren was more than up to the challenge. The bully easily avoided the overly committed fist and let Alex follow through and fall over again.

"What was that? My sister hits better," said Darren.

Alex, undeterred, got back on his feet and stood over Ian, fists up ready to swing again and protect his friend. "P–Piss off, Darren!"

"Oh, piss off is it?"

Darren marched forward and wrapped his big hand around Alex's throat. Pushing him backward, he slammed Alex hard against the nearest tree.

"If only your dad didn't work at the pit!"

Ian could have sworn he heard a cracking sound when Darren kicked him in the chest. He was also convinced a rib was broken, maybe even two. It was certainly really painful for a couple of seconds, that was for sure.

Now that he had time to gather his thoughts and compose himself a little, all he could feel now were pins and needles again. And he was pretty sure he could feel his ribs snap back into place. The blood that left his nose earlier seemed to be returning home too. A curious sensation, like drinking a milkshake through your nose.

Darren spied a nearby branch of the tree, and crawling on a leaf he saw a bright red ladybird[6]. The bug was busily conducting a full inspection of the leaf, probing the edges for a way down, possibly pondering whether to use its wings.

"That'll do," said Darren.

With his free hand, he reached up and used his thumb to push the ladybird off the leaf into the cup of his hand. "You hungry Alex?"

"Oh come on Darren, that's disgusting!"

"I know! But it won't leave a mark."

Darren shook his hand in order to keep the ladybird off-balance and grounded, using his other hand to grab Alex across the face. He pressed his thumb and fingers hard into Alex's cheeks to force his mouth open. Alex tried to push his hand

---

[6]   Also known as a ladybug, may bug, golden top, golden bug and even, bishy barabee, for some reason.

away, but Darren was putting all his considerable body weight behind the move, and Alex couldn't fight it.

"Open wide!"

Darren slammed the palm of his bug-carrying hand over Alex's wide open mouth, and the ladybird was catapulted right to the back of Alex's throat. This caused Alex to reflexively gulp and swallow the bug whole.

"Ha! How did that taste?"

"Let him go Darren," said Ian, who was now on his feet again.

"Oh, you're back," said Darren, slightly relieved Ian wasn't as badly hurt as he thought. "You best shut up or I'll hurt you proper."

"Let him go," said Ian.

"Why? I'm just helping Alex here with his breakfast."

Alex, while aware of his current predicament and glad to see that Ian was now up and about again, was processing something entirely new. He had just been forced to eat a ladybird, which he was surprised to note actually didn't taste of anything. A bigger concern right now however, was the sudden and weird pain he was feeling in his forehead and rib cage. Weird as in not horrible, but odd because it reminded him of growing pains, only way more intense and focused on specific areas of his head, torso, and now his skin.

As Alex processed that, his mind also started to picture the ladybird. Images of the bug, the robot surgeons, and the tall white room flashed through his mind. His body was being altered, getting new parts installed. Alex started to simply accept a new way of being, and he was convinced he needed a better read on his environment. To do that though, he would need to use his antennae. So out they popped, like the weasel. POP! POP! Two shiny black antennae sticking out of his forehead, tasting the air. *Nothing strange about that at all.*

An extra set of arms followed, shooting out from either side of his body. They tore through his old school shirt. Exact copies of the originals, sticking out from about half way down Alex's torso. *Nothing odd about that either.* As each new part arrived, he could feel pins and needles and intense heat rush to the area of the transformation, but also felt that something much bigger was happening. Deeper somehow. A sensation in his stomach. A pressure, like having gas but not being able to belch or fart.

Alex's new second set of limbs grabbed Darren's arms and pinned them to the bully's sides. Alex then effortlessly lifted the now speechless bully off the ground. Ian looked on, his mouth wide open. Darren kicked and struggled to escape but couldn't over-power Alex's incredibly firm grip.

As Alex's skin began to harden, he was equally fascinated by and accepting of his new look. His antennae tapped Darren's face and neck, sampling the bully's sweaty brow, giving Alex a complete picture of Darren's day so far. He knew Darren had had cornflakes that morning, with skimmed milk and lots of sugar. Darren had also drunk some orange juice and smoked a cigarette in the last two hours. The stench of the tobacco nearly overwhelmed Alex's newly acute senses.

"Let me go!" screamed a now petrified Darren. "PLEASE!"

"Ian," said Alex.

"Yes?"

"WHAT DO I DO NOW?"

"Err, I don't know. What do you want to do?" asked Ian.

"I don't know. I've never had the upper hand before!"

Darren continued to struggle. "Let me go!"

Alex effortlessly lifted the bully over his head and used his original set of hands to clamp Darren's face still.

"Okay Darren, I'm going to let you go. But you have to promise never to pick on us again. Got it?"

"Okay, I promise! Please stop staring at me. Please let me go!"

"Is that okay Ian?"

"Sounds good to me."

Alex wasn't convinced Darren got the message, but whether this bully turned over a new leaf or not was the last thing he needed to worry about at the moment. Perhaps one last show of force was needed.

Using all four arms, Alex gave Darren a gentle push and watched as the bully flew right over Ian's head. Darren landed on the ground approximately twenty feet away, and as quickly as he could, got to his feet and hobbled out of the woods.

CHAPTER 11

Boldly Going Ladybird!

The spring sun peeked out over the horizon, and started to broadcast its light over England's postcard-genic countryside. The grass covered hills surrounding Rossolington sparkled as the light refracted through a billion drops of morning dew. Mother Nature, once again made her grand entrance. She does like to show off.

The sun's light quickly reached the sleepy village. First colliding with Fullerton airport to the east, then heading over to Bishop Road and Bridge Lane, where it ricocheted off red brick houses with spotless windows into the connecting streets. Sneaking and spilling into people's gardens, living rooms and kitchens and dancing around empty milk bottles ready for collection before heading further in Rossolington and the woods behind York Street.

As the sun's energy reached the woods, a small ladybird began to stir as the temperature started to climb. After crawling out from under the leaf he was using for cover, he let the sun's warm light wash over his bright red wing covers. It was a vital part of his morning routine before taking on a full day of aphid hunting and looking for a proper lady ladybird with which to get acquainted.

The day before he sampled chemical chatter about a rich supply of juicy aphids in a large Ash tree in the woods, and had managed to reach the base of said tree before night-fall. Where there were aphids, he would also find some lovely females. Lots of food and good company, and the tree would provide cover from those woodland creatures who would like to call him "lunch."

But first, he had some climbing to do. He preferred to climb, all ladybirds did. He could deploy his wings and be in the thick of the tree in just a few seconds, but by doing so, he might miss important chatter laid down by the other creatures that called this place home. Even if he couldn't completely understand the chemical language, if there was something dangerous hiding behind the next branch, well, let's just say the trace left behind by the bug that just kicked the bucket was universally understood.

So off the ladybird went, carefully sampling as he marched up the largest exposed root to the base of the tree. He ignored gibberish ant chatter about formations, discipline and songs celebrating their queen, while taking special note of fellow ladybird news about local bird traffic, and the location of several spider webs left by those lucky enough to have escaped the twisted eight-legged freaks. He hated spiders more than most. Their eight legs and web building, only to sit and wait for dinner to come to them. It didn't seem right to the ladybird, even lazy, in a way.

Continuing his ascent, he climbed into one of the deeper ruts in the tree's bark. This line didn't look to have too many twists and turns and extended as far as the ladybird could see, giving him a nice quick highway to the first set of major branches, while hopefully providing some shaded cover. Damn his colourful eye-catching elytra[7].

He wasn't the first one to use this corridor, and the ladybird started to pick up a lot of useful information about the aphid population—this indeed was the tree everyone was spewing about. Unfortunately, he also picked up more ant chatter. The ladybird hated ants quite a lot too. Their militaristic nature, marching in single file. They polluted the communication channels with their queen worship and controlled massive herds of aphids to milk them. He thought they were creepy, and always tried to give them a wide berth. The ladybird knew he could handle one or two, but ants were smarter than they looked and liked to attack in large groups. If they got him on his back, he'd be dissected in a matter of seconds, and his quest for food and ladybird-right-now would be over.

As he reached the first set of major branches, he was focused on a specific trail. One left by a certain lady he had encountered before, though never directly abdomen to abdomen. Beautiful big thing she was—easily three times his size—with the brightest elytra he'd ever seen and four perfectly symmetrical spots, two on each wing cover. She was a vision, a foreigner, exotic and mysterious.

As he followed the trail onto the first major branch of the tree, the chatter in the air began to pick up. The entire wood suddenly went on high alert. Species after species sent out their message on the breeze: Inside-Outs! Inside-Outs!

The ladybird wasn't worried as he'd dealt with their kind before. They could be vicious and stupid, but mostly they

---

[7] Wing covers (el-i-tra). Red, orange or sometimes yellow, with a selection of black spots. Designed to make hungry predators think twice before eating them.

seemed curious. They were as big as a tree and could crush you without even knowing it, sure, but cowardly and easily spooked too. *Must be because their flesh is on the outside*, thought the ladybird. *They have no protection. Just walking around like that unshielded must be stressful*, he thought. *Hoping that thin sack they live in doesn't tear and everything falls out. What a horrible way to live.*

At that point, as the ladybird had almost reached the end of the branch, the entire tree shook. He looked down and saw that one of the Inside-Outs had smashed another into the tree. Fighting? Mating? He didn't really care, he just hoped the tree-quake hadn't disturbed his lunch and date plans, and he continued to follow the chemical trail to the last leaf on the branch.

Finally arriving at the leaf, he found the trail had stopped. In the last note his beloved had left, she had complained about the Inside-Outs. She had fallen off the leaf when the Inside-Outs crashed into the tree. The ladybird was beyond irritated, having travelled all that way for nothing. He couldn't even locate a single aphid for his trouble.

As the ladybird probed the edges of the leaf to get a good look around, he noticed one of the Inside-Outs was looking in his direction. The Inside-Out then reached up with one of its fleshy limbs to grab his leaf. Poop! It had seen him. Usually this wasn't a huge issue, as most of the time they just liked to watch you walk about on their dirty, hairy limbs and assault your senses with all the vile liquid pouring out from them. An unintelligible cocktail of chemicals made by all the nasty unnatural things it had consumed. The ladybird often wondered how these creatures lived past a week.

He didn't want any Inside-Out nonsense today. He was tired and hungry after his wasted journey and just wasn't in the mood. Time to deploy the wings—poop, too late!

The Inside Out pushed the ladybird off the leaf and held him captive. The fleshy cage he was in started to shake back and forth, making it impossible for the ladybird to get his footing long enough to lift his covers and deploy his wings.

Just when he thought he might have a second to make his escape, he felt a sudden and intense acceleration. The ladybird could see he was fast approaching what might be an Inside-Out's mouth.

Before he could do anything about it, he found himself forced into the mouth, landing at the back of the cavernous opening after bouncing off a disgusting, fleshy object hanging from the ceiling. The back of the moist cave then quickly closed in front of him, forcing him further into the Inside-Out. He slid down a wet tunnel and landed in a large, dank cave. Its moist surface overloaded his senses with chemical information.

First one, then another, then hundreds, no, thousands of tiny red lights appeared in the darkness. The ladybird could see an uncountable number of tiny insect-like creatures scurrying towards him. So tiny they were hard to see at first, but as they got closer, his very keen eyes could pick out more details. They had six legs but they weren't any kind of bug he'd seen before.

From all sides, the tiny red-eyed insects approached. Millions, no, billions of them now, crawled in and around and over each other, crashing over the ladybird like a wave. *This is it, the end*, thought the ladybird. His plans for a nice aphid dinner were gone and replaced by "the light" he'd heard about. The bright tunnel you see before you go to bug heaven. He'd not actually believed the stories, but couldn't argue with what he was seeing now. There it was, a bloody tunnel made of light. *Who knew?*

FLASH!

The ladybird still *felt* alive, but that was no proof he actually was. He'd been transported to a room with very few distinguishing features as far as he could make out. Some neatly arranged lights in the ceiling above him lit the area he currently occupied and he could just make out a raised platform at the far end of the space. He noticed he felt much heavier than before, which made it difficult to move. So far, he was not impressed with the afterlife.

Another light turned on and illuminated a dark corner of the room. This revealed a small creature. A strange looking thing, but a familiar shape. Like a large ant, but seemingly made from the same stuff as the tiny insects he had encountered inside the Inside-Out. It had a big head too, which supported two large, round eyes and a pair of stumpy antennae. The creature seemed to be asleep; its eyes were dark.

Suddenly, the creature's eyes flashed blue, then orange. The two colours appeared again, blue, then orange, blue, then orange. This got faster and faster until it was impossible to clearly see either colour, making the eyes appear a kind of back-lit brown. The rest of its body started to move, and it used its six legs to cartwheel across the room towards the raised platform. After waving one of its limbs, the platform lit up and the creature began rapidly wiggling its antennae to produce a coloured gas in response to the display. Each combination on the panel that was successfully matched by what the creature was excreting led to another round of coloured lights, and so on.

The ladybird, hungry and confused, quickly tired of the show and completely unimpressed by the service he was receiving beyond the grave, decided to lay down a strongly worded chemical complaint, when something new happened.

As he lay down something along the lines of "*Hey you, how about some bloody service!*", he noticed his chemical trail appeared as coloured spots in the air, similar to what the creature had been sending to the panel. They were bigger however, and moved quickly in all directions, a bright rainbow of dissatisfaction with the afterlife. It certainly seemed to do the trick though and the small creature jumped back and responded.

The ladybird was surprised and relieved to find he mostly understood the creature's chemical response. It certainly suggested surprise at the arrival of the ladybird, followed by a sentiment the ladybird currently shared.

"What the POOP!"

CHAPTER 12

Ladybird Boy!

"Ready?" asked Ian.

"Ready!" said Alex.

WHAM!

"Did you feel that?"

"No, not really. What I mean is, it didn't hurt."

Ian stepped in front of his friend holding a thick branch, which had partially splintered in the centre. "That's amazing, your back is rock hard."

"Like a beetle's?"

"Yeah, I guess so," said Ian. "And the way you just threw Darren, it's like—"

"Like I'm freakishly strong for my size? Like a beetle?"

"Right. How do you feel?"

"Like this is the most fantastic thing that's ever happened—ever!"

Alex paced back and forth excitedly, punching the air with all four fists. "I'm a freaking superhero! Bug Man! No, Beetle Man, no—"

"Ladybird Boy?" said Ian with a smirk of his face.

Alex locked a pair of shiny new black eyes on Ian and was not amused.

"Okay, don't stare at me with those, they're creepy."

Alex looked away and started to scan the trees. He'd never seen the woods like this before; the detail was amazing. If he focused, he could pick out a convoy of ants thirty feet away and his antennae sampled all sorts of weird bug chatter. The woods were alive and very aware of their presence; they were all *everything* was talking about.

"It's amazing. I think the bugs talk to each other, all the different kinds. Like different languages, and the words are in the air and on the dirt. Not something you hear, but taste."

Alex put his head close to the ground and tapped his antennae against the soil.

"I know ants have been here, and other ladybirds, earwigs, and spiders."

"Spiders?"

"Yeah, but don't worry. There's none nearby. Weird how I know that, right?"

"Oh, what's weird?" asked Ian. "I'm just standing in the woods bunking off school and my best friend has turned into a giant human-ladybird."

"Oh bollocks, yeah, school! Well, I can't go like this can I?"

"Err, no. I don't know what we do now. What's your mum going to say? You tore your shirt. She's going to be really mad."

"Really? You don't think she'll be more worried about these?"

Alex crisscrossed his four arms and let the upper and lower sets introduce themselves to each other with awkward backward handshakes.

"Fair point. Listen, I just had a thought. We both had the same dream last night and both of us had pins and needles after eating lunch. Do you think I'll turn into a ladybird if I ate one?"

"We could find one and see."

"I don't know. Sure it would be cool to have an extra set of hands, be super strong and indestructible. But what would my dad say? What would happen to us if the government found out? They always hunt down weird aliens to do experiments. We need to think about this. What if you're like this forever? What are people going to think? I mean, can you go home? Are you going to live in the woods?"

Alex stood up and took a fresh look at himself.

"I didn't think about it that way. My dad's going to go nuts. They'll make me live under the stairs and only let me out at night. Actually, that wouldn't be so bad since that's when crime fighters usually do their work. Right?"

At that point, Alex felt something stirring in his stomach, and then the pins and needles returned. "Hold on, something's happening."

"What?"

"It's my belly. Doesn't feel right."

Alex carefully sank to his knees and held his stomach with all four hands.

"What? Is it painful?"

"Yeah, it's indigestion or something. And my tongue, it feels like I just ate iron filings."

Alex winced as his symptoms got worse and he curled up into a ball on the ground.

"What'll I do?" asked Ian. "Shall I get your mum?"

Alex reached out and grabbed Ian's leg.

"No, wait a second. It's getting better. Oh wow, that feels funny."

Alex jumped to his feet with his four arms extended, his antennae standing tall. Then, one by one, his eyes cleared and returned to their slightly blueish-grey selves, and his antennae were sucked back into his head as quickly as they had popped out. The arms followed, one at a time pulling themselves back into his body. Like he was made of clay, and the sculptor was moulding the material back into his torso.

After the quick restoration, Alex inspected his forehead and torso, and could find no marks on his skin. "It's like it never happened. Stomach still tingles though."

"You look normal. Taller than when you were a ladybird too."

"I'm taller?"

"Yeah. Makes sense, I guess. Like parts of your body were used to make the extra bits, so you got shorter."

"Really? Does any of this make sense? How long do you reckon I was a ladybird?"

"My guess, twenty minutes, maybe."

Alex put his left hand on his belly. "I don't think I'm finished yet."

"Really? What's happening now?"

"You know what? I think I need to fart!"

And then it happened. A prolonged, approximately fifteen-second-long performance from Alex's tailpipe, the built up emissions after the "engine" of his transformation had completed its task. A truly awesome event that sounded like the most vigorous drum roll you could imagine performed on a very large wet fish. Loud and incredibly stinky, polluting the woods around them with a smell you'd expect from a poop salad with sewage dressing.

A horrified Ian backed away from his friend in a hurry. "Oh urgh, that's RANK!"

Alex, somewhat relieved, found the event actually quite funny and started to giggle. "Wow, that was a good one!"

After the boys had waved the noxious gas away, they collected their school bags and walked back the entrance to the woods.

"Twenty minutes is perfect. I can eat a ladybird, and get superpowers for twenty minutes, fight crime, and then return back to normal before I go home for tea."

"Are you serious? Fight crime? What crime? This is Rossolington. Nothing ever happens here. Plus, how do you know it'll work again? And what about other bugs? What about me?"

Alex and Ian left the woods and started down Oxford Street.

"You're right, we need to do some tests after tea today. Collect as many bugs as you can and we'll meet in the den to do some experiments," said Alex.

The boys reached Darren's house and looking down at them from his bedroom window was their beaten bully. Clearly shaken with a blank expression on his face, he stared at Alex and Ian, and they stared back at him.

"Do you think he'll say anything?" asked Ian.

"What would he say?"

"Good point. Think we'll be bothered by him again?"

"I don't think so, somehow."

Alex took two fingers and pointed at his eyes, and then pointed a single finger straight at Darren. The universal signal for "I've got my eyes on you!"

Darren stepped back away from the window and closed the curtains.

Ian and Alex chuckled as they continued on to school.

"Oh my God, I can't believe you did that!" said Ian.

CHAPTER 13

Nice or nice?

Mike Ridley's mind was being forced to work overtime and he wasn't happy about it.

After Tuesday's shift at the pit, his head was filled with images spinning in circles as if fed into an old View-Master 3D toy, operated by a sugared-up child trying to see how fast he can make the wheel turn. From Mr. Brock's piles of bonus cash to Samantha's holiday brochures and Frank's defaced parking sign, his head was a manic gallery of expectations—time for a pint.

Rossolington had two public houses located across the street from each other in the centre of the village. The aptly named Black Lung workman's club, set up exclusively for the miners by their union, and the more family friendly, White Rose. And by family friendly, that meant they offered food, and by food, that meant they could deftly microwave a selection of "food" type items. Mystery meat burgers, potato-like fries, or their specialty, pepperoni-looking pizza, which made Mrs. Brock's sausage rolls look almost edible. All overpriced and usually over microwaved (to be safe), yet incredibly popular with the punters after an evening of beer and more beer.

Mike, not in the mood for a zapped mystery meal, popped into The Black Lung. It was a large establishment, once Rossolington's only school before it was closed down and converted. A simple watering hole where a miner could enjoy a cheap pint, and unwind with his peers after a hard day's graft.

The former school's main hall was set up with several long A-Frame picnic tables arranged into neat rows with the large bar built against the back wall, opposite the main stage. A perfect set up for an evening of booze fuelled dancing and musical entertainment. And by musical entertainment, that meant Friday night's inevitable drunken battle over the karaoke machine to see who got to sing Tammy Wynette's, "Stand by Your Man."

Mike took his belly to the bar, ordered a pint, drank it quickly, belched, then ordered another. As the club started to fill up, Mike settled into the warm atmosphere with some of his mates from the pit. He breathed in the smoke-filled air and stench of beer and enjoyed a few belly laughs as everyone loosened up and started to tell the latest jokes they'd heard.

One round lead to another, and then another. No one was going to be the guy who didn't get in a round, so it wasn't long before Mike and his group were singing songs and telling old stories. But try as he might, Mike wasn't able to fully commit to the evening's debauchery. Partially because it was a school night and he had work the next day, but mostly because his cell phone wouldn't leave him alone. If it wasn't Donald Brock texting him pictures of money, it was Samantha's ever louder voicemail messages asking about his whereabouts.

Unable to take full advantage of Black Lung's comforting atmosphere or the round he was now owed (logged in the mental beer ledger for next time), Mike begrudgingly decided to cut his night short, and stagger home.

The reception once he got there, was less than friendly.

Samantha, a stout woman, sat at the dining room table not-so-gently beating her left hand with a rolling pin. In front of her sat an entire travel shops collection of holiday ideas, all neatly arranged and ever present to make sure Mike never forgot his seemingly single duty in this marriage—to provide Samantha with one decent vacation per year.

Mike wasn't an idiot and right away could see Samantha was disappointed, which was bad because disappointed was a hundred times worse than angry. Angry he could handle. Angry was a shouting match and maybe a night on the sofa. Disappointed, on the other hand, could be the end of everything. So, knowing he would have to be very careful, he sat down across the table from her and tried to think through the booze. Piecing together the first words that bubbled to the surface to form any kind of coherent sentence that might appease this tiny, powerful ball of dissatisfaction.

"Err, listen Sammy."

Samantha stiffened. *Okay, we're beyond using pet names*, thought Mike.

"Listen. I was coming home, but I had a rough day and then Mr. Brock's new assistant gave me funny looks—"

Samantha stopped beating the palm of her hand with the rolling pin and glared at Mike. He replayed the last sentence in his head, realized why that might be the last thing he should start with, and quickly scrambled to the subject of money, Samantha's favourite.

"I mean, I went to see Donald, and he had all these big piles of cash on his desk. Which he said were mine."

Samantha seemed to ease a little, and returned to DEFCON 4[8].

"But only if we fill our quota on time. The problem is, Frank has shut down the new seam because it's unsafe, so I don't see how we can—"

DEFCON 3 again. Samantha knew who Frank was, and had had dealings with Sharon in the past. Kind of a hate-hate thing. She hated the cash flow interruptions Frank caused in the name of safety, and Sharon's accursed Angel-cakes were always a hit at the annual miner's Christmas party instead of her over baked jam-tarts. Which traditionally ended up being used as replacement pucks by the kids on the large air hockey table in the miner's rec room.

"But, I may have an idea how we might get around this," said Mike, looking up at the ceiling for inspiration. "Err, if I could somehow get Frank out of the mine for a couple of weeks, I could get the quota mostly filled. By the time Frank got back, I'd have the support structures in place, and we'd be able to continue with Frank's blessing."

DEFCON 4.

Mike was tired and sobering up faster than he liked. His stupor was on the verge of becoming a buzz, and was marching quickly towards Headache Town. He decided to use his last remaining card.

---

8   One step away from a rolling pin upgrade to Mike's Cricket bat (3), and one setting above peace in our time (5).

"Frank would be pissed off we worked the seam, and there'd likely be consequences, but I'd at least get the big bonus."

He scanned the brochures in front of him, and luckily spied one advertising France. He reached across the table, picked it up, and turned it towards Samantha.

"And, if I get that big bonus, well? How about a nice trip to the South of France?"

DEFCON 5. Alert the Pentagon, call the Prime Minister, we have reached DEFCON 5. Samantha stopped batting the rolling pin against her palm, slowly stood up, and walked into the kitchen. Mike watched on in terror, adjusting his seating position to better facilitate a move if he suddenly had to dive out of the path of an angry condiment bottle.

Mike instead, however, heard a familiar sound of metal popping, followed by a brief hiss of gas.

Samantha walked back over to Mike and placed a nice cold can of lager in front of him, then gently kissed his cheek. She reached over to the brochure he had selected before, opened it to a page she had previously marked, and pointed at the package deal advertised. A full two weeks in Nice.

"Nice?" said Mike.

"No Mikey, Nice," said Samantha.

Time to Experiment!

Tuesdays at Robin Bank Academy were worse than Mondays, a day that started with maths and English literature ('lit', if trying to sound cool), and an afternoon filled with humiliating physical education exercises. Starting with a simple yet exhausting game of British Bulldog[9], followed by a violent and confidence-destroying round of dodge ball.

This Tuesday, however, was a little different for Alex and Ian. Despite itching to get back to the woods to experiment with Alex's new superpowers, the two boys were happy to discover a whole new angle on school life.

---

[9] British Bulldog. A large group of kids stand on one side of the playground, while a single child stands in the center. On commencement of the game, the group of children run to the other side, avoiding the child in the middle. The lone hunter in this scenario must grab anyone he/she can, and hold onto them until they can shout, one, two, three British Bulldog. Their new prisoner then joins them in the center, and the larger group tries once again to cross the playground. The winner is the last kid left uncaptured.

First period's math class was usually spent at the back of the room, hunkered down using one hand to support the head and shield the eyes against any potentially disastrous eye contact with Mrs. Jones. The theory being, if you couldn't see her, she couldn't see you, and you wouldn't end up in front of the class trying to solve a difficult math problem.

Today was different. Alex and Ian were competing to see who could raise their hand quicker and higher to get the correct answer first, much to the amazement of Mrs. Jones and the rest of the class.

English lit (see, it is cooler) was a breeze too. Being asked to read in front of the class was usually akin to being asked if you'd like to fall off a cliff. But today, both Alex and Ian volunteered to read the school mandated Shakespearean material and they both nailed it. At one point they even started to act out Romeo's conversations with Mercutio— "a plague on both your houses!" —resulting in a hardy round of applause from everyone in the room. Including teachers and kids from neighbouring classrooms that heard the commotion and decided to catch the show.

Alex and Ian were unstoppable.

The game of British Bulldog saw tides turn in the unwritten hierarchy of the school yard too. Both Alex and Ian saw out the entire exercise uncaptured, effortlessly running rings around other kids in the class, even the so called "athletes." They challenged and destroyed the competition, even seeming to get faster as the afternoon wore on. In the end it became clear to everyone that the only person who could catch Ian was Alex, and Alex was the only one that could hit Ian with the dodge ball.

Best day at school, ever.

Word of their newfound confidence and abilities spread quickly, and before they knew it, they started to pick up an entourage. Kids that didn't even know they existed were now asking for help with maths and inviting them to join the school soccer team. Their newfound fame also started to attract girls, a first for both boys, and it was the only time during the day they felt their confidence wane. As they recalled, no robot arm in their dreams swapped out their brains or installed new software explaining—girls. Perhaps these creatures were meant to remain enigmas? Alex and Ian just bought them sweets from the school tuck shop[10]. That seemed to appease them, and it was a lot easier than talking.

When the final bell rang, the boys were glad the school day was over. Being celebrities was exciting, but also exhausting and a lot to process. They also had more interesting work to do, and the boys agreed to meet at their hideout in the woods right after tea.

Alex and Ian's den consisted of a loose collection of old doors arranged like playing cards, using a large Oak tree for support. It employed a tatty old tarp for the roof, which sagged and collected water every time it rained.

Inside the den, the boys had furnished their home away from home with an old dressing table and a moth-eaten sofa. The place also had its own toilet, which both Alex and Ian agreed should only be used for emergency number ones. They had once discussed digging a deep hole underneath their convenience to make it more useful, but in the end decided it was too much work and too disgusting to think about. As much as they loved having their well-hidden secret base in the woods, it was always far nicer to take care of number twos at home near some nice, soft toilet paper.

---

[10] The school's shop, selling all manner of unhealthy sugar-filled biscuits and sweets.

Alex arrived first, carrying a tiny paper bag containing his collection of bugs harvested during his epic day at school. A pathetic collection, which said as much about the amount of time Alex had available to secretly collect dead insects as it did about his dislike of bugs. He arranged them in a row on the dressing table. Three flies, one slightly squished ladybird with a broken wing, and an earwig that didn't have its pincers anymore.

Looking at his collection again, Alex wasn't excited about the evening's experiments.

At that point Alex heard a rustling in the bushes near the entrance to the den and called out. "Who goes there?"

"It's me, ya berk," said Ian.

"Okay, just checking."

Ian appeared at the entrance of the den carrying a large cardboard box and walked over to the dresser. "Is that your collection?" asked Ian, referring to Alex's mini-buffet of deceased insects.

"Yeah, so? That's all I could find."

"Pitiful." With a single swipe, Ian brushed them off the dressing table and set his box down. Alex's rejected bugs disappeared inside the boxes filled with the boy's collection of dead electronic parts they liked to disassemble from time to time.

"Hey, it took me all day to collect those! I even found a ladybird."

Ian just looked at Alex and smiled, then he pointed to his box. "You want to see a real collection?"

Alex rolled his eyes, sat down on the sofa and watched as Ian started arranging match boxes and small brown medicine jars on the table. Alex could hear scratching noises coming from within the small cardboard boxes and could just make out the shapes of ants and earwigs crawling around their new glass prison cells.

"Bloody hell! When did you find time to collect those?"

"After school. I emptied out these old boxes and bottles I was using for my technical Lego and found all these bugs in my front yard."

Ian handed a clipboard to Alex. "Here, hold onto this. We'll need to record everything we try."

Alex started to rifle through the papers clamped to the board. Each page had been labelled with the name of a particular type of bug at the top of the paper, and then both Alex's and Ian's names were spaced out down the left hand side to leave room for notes.

"Wow, you're taking this seriously."

"Aren't you? I thought you wanted to be a superhero."

"I do. But all this? We're really going to eat bugs?"

"Looks that way." Ian finished arranging his collection of bottles and boxes on the table and then turned to Alex to retrieve his clipboard. "Okay we're ready. Take off your shirt."

"WHAT?"

"Take off your shirt. You ripped the last one. Did your mum freak out?"

"Err, I told my mum I ripped it during Bulldog. She didn't seem to mind though which was weird. Mum and dad were talking all through tea. My dad's going away for a couple of weeks for some business trip. My dad thinks Mr. Brock, the pit boss, is up to something."

"Lucky break for you about the shirt. But let's not push your luck and rip another. Take it off."

Alex rolled his eyes again. "What about you?"

"Later. We're starting with you first."

Ian looked at the first page on his clipboard, and then turned to his collection and picked up a small matchbox labelled "ladybird." He slid the tiny drawer open and picked out one of the dead bugs. "Here you go," said Ian placing the small creature in the palm of Alex's hand.

Alex looked at it for a few seconds, its little legs curled up, lying on its back.

"Just do what Darren did. Throw it back there and swallow," said Ian, who reached back into his box and produced a small bottle of water. "You can wash it down with this. Like a pill."

"I hate taking pills."

Alex grabbed the bottle of water, then threw the tiny bug into his mouth and washed it down with some water. "Urgh!"

"Did it taste bad?" asked Ian.

"Not really, if I'm honest; it's not like I wanted to chew on it and find out. Just the thought of it, you know? Its little legs inside my belly." Alex shuddered.

The two boys waited and Alex stepped back in preparation of his transformation, but nothing happened.

"It was pretty quick before. How do you feel?" asked Ian.

"I feel nothing. Last time, it was like growing pains and pins and needles, and fast. Boom, I'm part bug and holding Darren above my head."

Ian fished out another dead ladybird from his matchbox and handed it to Alex. "Go on, try again."

"No. You try."

"Fair enough," said Ian, and he threw the tiny creature straight into his mouth like a mint.

The boys waited again, but nothing. Ian grabbed his clipboard and pen, and started to write down the results. "Alex, Ian, one dead ladybird each. Nothing happened."

Alex slumped back onto the sofa, a little disappointed that he wasn't going to be ladybird boy. Ian put his matchbox and clipboard back on the dressing table and picked up a small bottle. "Care for an ant?"

"What? You want to eat an ant now? I'm starting to think you're enjoying this," said Alex.

"I think I am. I've read about all these countries that eat insects, like Thailand and Ghana. Seems to work okay for them, so why not?"

"Because it's disgusting, and this is England. We eat chips, fish, curry, and Yorkshire puddings."

"I know, boring. So you're saying no to the ant then?"

"Yes. You go for it."

Ian carefully unscrewed the lid of the bottle, and let a couple of the ants crawl out.

"Oh my God you're going to eat a live one?"

"Sure. Don't ask me why, but I had a feeling the dead bugs wouldn't work. I think they have to be alive. The first ladybird you ate was alive when you swallowed it."

Alex cupped his head in his hands and groaned. "You have no idea how much I hope you're wrong about that."

Ian carefully let the ants crawl onto one hand and with the other reached for the bottle of water.

"I figured ants would be a solid choice for powers, if this even works, of course. Ants can lift their own weight several times over. They're fast, tough, and easy to find. They should also survive the trip to my stomach, even if I wash them down with some water."

Ian started to snap at the ants scurrying around his hand, but getting one to stay still long enough to be gobbled up proved to be difficult. Ian repeatedly twisted his hand around, trying to anticipate each ant's direction. Eventually, though, he got his timing right as one of the ants headed to the top of one of his fingers. Snap! In the mouth it went, closely followed by a mouthful of water.

Alex cringed. "Is something happening?"

"Oh dear," said Ian, smiling. "I forgot to take off my shirt."

<u>Notes</u>: Ant

<u>Ian</u>: Ate 1 ant. Powers – extra arms, really, really strong, tough skin, antennae and wall crawling!

<u>Alex</u>: Accidentally ate 2 ants (berk!) Powers – the same as me. The extra ant made no difference.

<u>Side effects</u>: Less stomach pain than the ladybird, but the fart afterward was epic! Sounded like molten lava landing on bubble wrap!

<u>Notes</u>: Grasshopper

<u>Ian</u>: Ate 1. Powers – Extra arms. Legs got really long and I could jump over the biggest trees in the wood. Arms not as strong as when I was an ant, and it was difficult to walk and run with those legs. Good eyes and sense of smell, and really long antennae.

<u>Alex</u>: Ate 1 really small grasshopper. Powers – same as me, only not as much. Size matters.

<u>Side effects</u>: Some stomach pain, and lots of gas. Farts sounded like a rattlesnake's tail. Really smelly, too!

Notes: Earwig

Ian: Ate 1 earwig. Powers – Extra arms and antennae, tough skin and strong, but the pincers appeared just above our bums. Not sure how much use they'll be back there.

Alex: Earwig bit his tongue so he spat it out. We're going to assume he'd get the same powers I did.

Side effects: Bad stomach pain. Fart sounded like jelly skipping across a pond.

Notes: Fly

Ian: Ate 1. Powers – Yes yes yes! Wings! I can fly! Brilliant! Really fast in the air too. Got extra arms, but didn't feel strong. Could wall crawl though.

Alex: Ate 1, but he accidentally pulled the wings off his. So no flying. Everything else was the same. We've got to make sure the bugs are swallowed alive AND intact!

Side effects: We've timed the transformation and it seems to only last for just under 20 minutes. Must remember to be on the ground when the powers wear off! Will start wearing a watch to time the changes. Fart noise with the fly sounded like a spitfire shooting water balloons.

CHAPTER 15

The Nest and the Secti

The Milky Way is a spiral galaxy because from the top (relatively speaking), it looks like a spiral[11]. Like someone or something had unplugged the cosmic bathtub and all the stars and planets were slowly being sucked down the galactic drain. Including the planet Earth and all the little humans on it (located about half way between two arms of this spiral formation), and the planet known to its inhabitant's as the Nest, which lived nearby[12].

The Nest was a big planet. You could use the Earth to play tennis, and go ten-pin bowling with The Nest. It closely orbited its Red Giant star fast enough to make a year (again, relatively speaking) last 156 days, and it spun on its axis at such a rate as to make a day last twenty-one hours. A peaceful and

---

[11] Nothing gets by these scientific types!

[12] And by nearby, we mean really far away. As in, if you had an image of the galaxy printed on a letter sized piece of paper then yes, the Nest and Earth were "close". But if you were planning a spacewalk between the two planets, you had better set aside about 16,512,639,840 years for your journey.

lush planet in a distant part of the galaxy inhabited by a race of beings called the Secti.

Two of these Secti were very confused about the sudden arrival of a ladybird, three ants, two grasshoppers, and an earwig. Or, as they quickly became known, "the rude, spotted one, the cry-baby drones who couldn't stop singing about their queen, the ones with the hilarious legs, and the mean one with the pincers."

"Something else is coming through," signalled Portal Operator Pale Green with a chemical squirt and wiggle from his stumpy antennae.

"Oh, please not another one of those things with the pincers, they have anger issues!" spewed his exasperated Client Success Director, Orangey Blue.

The two Secti cowered behind their workstation as they awaited the imminent new arrival on the portal floor in front of them. Behind them, an impromptu zoo of the Nest's new alien visitors was loudly excreting their dissatisfaction with the treatment they had received after arriving.

"Where are these grumpy creatures coming from anyway?" asked Orangey Blue.

"Our trace has them entering two separate portals approximately 120 light years away. Both portals are located on a little planet somewhere between the arms."

"We have portals that far out?"

"Not that I know of. Perhaps one of the older missions finally became active somehow?"

At that point, a light flashed above the portal and their latest visitor appeared. Orangey Blue shook his bulbous head in disappointment.

"Oh, well, isn't that wonderful, this one flies!"

Administrator Reddish Brown paced back and forth on the ceiling of his office. "So how many have come through? …. Nine? And how are our new visitors? …. Angry huh? Well, I guess that's understandable, they've travelled a long way."

Reddish Brown released his hold on the ceiling and gracefully fell to the floor. He then smoothly cartwheeled over to the opening behind his workstation to survey "the network."

The Secti home world was made up of billions of hexagonal-shaped city hubs that were connected to each other via ten lane information highways. Each set of three hubs framed a large garden to create one city block, which was then connected by another highway to the next one, and so on. A design only interrupted by the planet's many mountain ranges and rivers. It was organized and beautiful, especially at night.

A blizzard of twinkling lights glowed as the citizens of the Nest went about their business. Their chemical chatter reacted to the trace amounts of hydrogen peroxide in the atmosphere producing a vibrant rainbow of colours. Transferring their consciousness between available host bodies at the speed of light, completely unaware that an ancient research project had suddenly started to yield results. Perhaps delivering a blast from their own past and signalling a huge shift in their understanding of the universe. They were not alone.

Administrator Reddish Brown turned towards his workstation and waved one of his arms to pull up holographic images of the planet's new arrivals, who were being held at the Secti's most remote portal location. "Client Success Director Orangey Blue. These are our guests and I want them treated well. They'll likely need to eat… Yes, eat, you know, food? …Like a power infusion only the power is converted internally through the consumption and breakdown of organic matter…Yes, I know it sounds disgusting… Just escort them to the gardens, I'm confident they'll find something to maintain their systems. Thank you, Orangey Blue."

The administrator flicked his left antenna to end the call, and then waved away the holographic images. He double tapped his workstation and a control panel appeared. "Time to inform the Nest."

Reddish Brown wiggled his antennae and a collage of coloured shapes appeared in the air and settled on the controls, which promptly sampled the administrator's emissions and responded with a single flashing green circle. Message received, understood—sending.

The administrator once again looked out over the network as the mix of colours in the cities started to settle on mostly green. It wouldn't be long before the entire planet knew everything about their new visitors. As much as Administrator Reddish Brown could show it, he was genuinely excited about the discovery of a planet ruled by creatures very similar to the Secti's ancestors.

A day later, Reddish Brown transferred his consciousness to an available host near the remote portal, and then cartwheeled into the garden to pay their guests a visit. Since it was his department and portal sector that welcomed the foreign dignitaries, it was his honour to conduct the first proper interviews. He couldn't wait to hear the wisdom of that bygone era. He was so excited that it was difficult to modulate the power flowing through his circuits. He decided to approach the first visitor to the planet, who was chewing on a sugar vine, one of the many variants of sweet plant life native to the Nest.

"You got any aphids?" asked the ladybird rudely before Reddish Brown could squirt out a single question.

"Umm, I don't think so. What's an aphid?"

"Small, squishy creature, tastes like an unripe apple."

"It's a living creature?"

"Sure, six legs, antennae, tiny head, a bit stupid. The ants were asking too," said the ladybird, and he leaned in closer to the administrator. "They like to milk them."

"Milk aphids?" asked Reddish Brown in horror.

"I know, right? Weird. You had better keep an eye on those ants. Once they realize her royal egg-layer-ness isn't here, they're likely to lose their little minds and start attacking everybody."

Reddish Brown looked over ladybird's wing covers at the three ants marching in single file across the garden. The leader was leaving a trail of directions for the other two ants to follow, and all three of them were tagging everything in the garden, "the property of her royal highness."

"Do you know where you are?" asked Reddish Brown.

The ladybird thought about that for a moment. "This is the afterlife. Right?"

"The afterlife? You mean you think you're dead and this garden is some sort of waiting area before you receive judgement?"

"Well it looks like it. There's no aphids, but there's plenty to eat. Haven't seen any birds or spiders since I've been here either, or Inside-Outs."

"I'm sorry, what are Inside-Outs?"

"Oh, they're horrible, huge things. As tall as a tree. We call them Inside-Outs because all their squishy stuff is on the outside."

"And these Inside-Outs, they're your servants?"

"Servants? Heck no. They're in charge. Weird creatures, stranger than ants and sneakier than spiders. They build massive stone structures, kill us indiscriminately, and destroy our homes."

Administrator Reddish Brown frantically wiggled his antennae over his workstation to record his notes after conducting lengthy interviews with each of the visiting insects. He was outraged by the treatment of his ancestors by these so-called "Inside-Outs" and ready to jump over to their home world and kick some squishy butt. His interviews logged eye witness accounts of cruel Inside-Out behaviour. Tales of torture as limbs were slowly removed, or entire colonies destroyed with chemical weapons. One of their visitors wasn't even allowed through the portal until the horrible monsters had viciously torn off its wings!

He was, however, confused about how their new visitors had made it to the Nest. So Reddish Brown had to wonder. Where exactly was the portal and what did these evil Inside-Outs want it for?

There was only one way to find out. It was time to assemble a team and visit the Inside-Out's home world.

CHAPTER 16

The Bug Boys

Ian strolled into the woods behind York Street. Alex had called him on his walkie-talkie and asked him to visit their super-secret superhero lair. They had completed a series of experiments and established a list of powers they could use. Flying, super strength, super hearing, super smell, and wall crawling. They were superheroes now, just like the ones in their favourite comic books, but they didn't have a cause or a crime to fight. The next step would be to pick a name for themselves and put their new abilities to good use somehow.

Rossolington, however, was hardly a hot bed of criminal activity. There were no robberies, beatings, shootings, or big crime bosses that would be worthy of the attention of two super-powered humans. Even Rossolington's own police force had very little to do. Constables Walker and Smith seemed to spend most days working on their waist lines while playing Solitaire on their computers at the police station.

There might be more action in larger towns nearby, but they would be more difficult to patrol, given the limited amount of time the two boys could be away from home. They also had no access to any equipment that could monitor police radio frequencies, so the notion that they would be able to find and then stop crime county wide seemed unlikely.

"What took you so long?" asked Alex, clearly eager to explain why he requested the meeting.

"Nothing. Just wasn't in a hurry. Thinking about what we can do now that we're superheroes."

"Ah, well, think no more because I know exactly what we're going to do." Alex pointed to a large box on the dressing table.

"We're going to stare at a box?" asked Ian.

"Ha. Ha. No. You did such a great job collecting the bugs, I thought I would match that with," Alex paused a little for dramatic effect, "costumes!"

Ian lunged for the box, but Alex blocked his path.

"Hold your horses, fellow superhero friend. Sit down, and let me show you what I put together."

Ian sat down on the sofa and Alex removed the lid to his box.

"So, first, I figured we'd need to be covered up, but we also need room for the arms and wings. Right?"

"Right," said Ian.

"So how about this?"

Alex presented an orange safety vest, the kind that was designed to cover a person's regular clothes to give them more visibility. It had thin elastic straps on either side connecting the two sections together, and two reflective stripes running front to back on either side. The left breast pocket had 'BB' painted on it in black paint. Alex turned the vest to show off the back, revealing the large, neat rectangular hole he cut near where the shoulder blades would be. "That hole is for the wings."

Ian jumped up off the sofa. "That's brilliant. Where did you get these?"

"My dad's old safety gear. They're a bit big, but," Alex excitedly reached into the box again, "we can use these to hold the vests in place at the waist."

Alex presented his friend with a leather belt, which had some of Ian's matchboxes and medicine bottles glued to it on the right hand side of the buckle. The bottoms of each matchbox were capped with a small piece of cardboard taped into place to prevent the drawers sliding downwards. The tops of each drawer and the bottle caps had tiny holes poked into them to let their bug collection breath.

"A utility belt?" asked Ian.

"A utility belt," said Alex, clearly very proud of his arts and crafts project. "We can keep all the different insects in these containers so they'll be available when we need them. We can even have some containers for plasters and stuff. Like a mini first aid kit."

Ian grabbed the vest from Alex and put it on. Since it was meant for a fully grown man, it was like wearing a small tent. The bottom of the vest was several inches below Ian's waist. He took the belt from Alex and tied it around his waist over the vest to see how it would look. Alex, meanwhile, dove back into the box to get his outfit.

"This is awesome!" said Ian.

Alex put on his vest and belt. "Yeah, thanks, it worked out pretty good, I think."

Ian looked down at his vest again. "What's 'BB' stand for?"

Alex again paused for dramatic effect. "Bug Boys!"

Ian stared back at his friend, and didn't say a word.

"Come on, Bug Boys? What's wrong with that? It's got a nice ring to it and it's accurate," said Alex.

"Alex," said Ian. "It's perfect!"

"Oh, okay, phew. You had me worried there. Anyway, we're not done; take a look inside the box."

Ian looked, and then smiled. He reached in and pulled out two dust masks. He handed one to Alex and then put on his own. The dust masks also had "BB" painted on them.

"You've thought of everything," Ian said, sounding slightly muffled under the mask.

Alex put his mask on. "Well, we'll want to protect our secret identities, and this was the simplest solution I could come up with that didn't get in the way of the transformations. This stuff is easy to replace too. My dad's got lots of it lying around."

Ian adopted the classic fists on hips superhero pose. "The Bug Boys, patrolling the streets of Rossolington. Ever alert, ready to serve Queen and country."

Alex joined in and started pacing dramatically around the lair. "Wherever evil lurks, the Bug Boys will be there, ready with their trusty supply of fresh insects!"

Ian laughed, and slumped down onto the sofa. Alex joined him.

"We still have one problem, though," said Ian, "no crimes to fight."

Alex stood up and removed his mask. "Well, I had an idea about that and I think I've got two missions we can do."

"Really? What?"

Alex removed his utility belt and safety vest and put them back in the box. "Well, for one, I wanted to help my dad with something. He's always thought his boss was stealing from the pit but doesn't have any proof. What if we raided his boss's office and nicked all his paperwork?"

Ian shifted uncomfortably on the sofa.

"You want to break into his office at the pit and steal paperwork? I thought we were going to fight crime."

"We are. My dad's never wrong; if he thinks his boss is stealing from the pit, then he's stealing from the pit. We would just be collecting evidence, like Batman does. We sneak in, collect all we can and then leave it somewhere for my dad to find. He can do the rest."

"I don't know, Alex. Seems a bit risky to me."

Alex sat back down on the sofa. "It'll be fine. We can approach the pit from the woods, and then use—" Alex smiled, "—our spider powers to climb into the boss's office."

"Spider powers?"

Alex pointed to one of the matchboxes on Ian's utility belt. "Open that one."

Ian looked nervously down at his utility belt and tried to suck in his gut to create some distance between himself and the spider crawling around inside the matchbox.

"It's okay," said Alex. "Go ahead and open it."

Ian slowly unbuckled his belt and held it out at arm's length. He then gingerly opened the box Alex pointed at and carefully looked inside to find a small brown capsule.

"I nicked some of my mum's multi-vitamins. I figured we could handle the bugs we really don't like by putting them inside these empty containers."

Alex picked up the capsule and held it up against a beam of light sneaking into their lair between the tarp and doors. The silhouette of a small, and likely very irritated, spider could be seen pacing back and forth. "Want to try it out?"

Ian reached over and took the capsule from Alex.

"But you have to promise to help me help my dad."

Ian stood up and walked over to the back of the lair to give himself space for the transformation. Alex and Ian had wanted to try spiders from the start, but just couldn't bring themselves to let the nasty things crawl all over their hands, let alone swallow one.

He took off his vest and then removed his shirt. Once that was done, he put the vest and belt back on, leaving the sides of his torso exposed for whatever transformation might occur.

"Well, okay. But then we focus on proper crimes to fight. How did you get the spider in here, anyway?"

"It wasn't easy," said Alex. "I had to first trap it in the bigger part of the capsule, and then put the pieces together before it could escape. It took five goes. Luckily this spider wasn't very big or fast. There's water in the box, too, if you need it."

Ian grabbed a bottle of water and eyed the capsule one more time. "Oh well, here goes."

Alex silently counted to himself, one, two, three, four, as Ian waited for vitamin spider to take effect. In their experiments, they had noticed a raw bug would cause the transformation within seconds. Now that they had to wait for the capsule to dissolve, they would need to record how long it took for the powers to kick in. Twenty-one, twenty-two, twenty-three, twenty-four.

"This should be cool," said Ian as he lifted his arms. "What do you think, four more arms?"

Thirty-five, thirty-six, thirty-seven, thirty-eight.

"And web slinging! I've always wanted to be able to do that."

Fifty-five, fifty-sex, fifty-seven.

"Oh," said Ian. "Here we go!"

Fifty-eight.

As Ian had suspected, two extra arms shot out from either side of his torso. As before with their other experiments, these were exact copies of his original set, and Ian instantly *knew* about each of them. They were as much a part of him as the original set was. Then his eyes changed and became shiny and black. They were joined by six more eyes of varying sizes which rose out of his forehead. Ian looked around the lair. "Oh wow, this is brilliant. It's like having eyes in the back of my head. I can almost see everything in the lair."

"How do you feel?" asked Alex.

"Good. Not really feeling strong like I did with the ant, but maybe we just need to use bigger spiders."

"Yeah, right. Bigger spiders. How about the webs?"

Ian smiled. "Right. Let's give that a try. Somehow I know how to shoot them, I'm just not sure what it's going to be like."

Ian held out his original left arm and pressed his middle fingers into the palm of his hand. The classic "I'm about to shoot webs" pose established in Ian's favourite comic books. Ian gave his wrist a flick to shoot the web.

Three things happened. Firstly, no webbing shot out from his wrist as his comic books had described. Secondly, Alex started to roll around on the floor laughing, tears streaming down his face. Lastly, it dawned on him that real life spiders don't shoot webs from their legs, and this was followed by a sinking feeling as he started to put two and two together. *Where do spiders shoot web from? Their spinnerets*, thought Ian. *What's the closest thing I have to that? MY BUM!*

Ian stood, disappointed and now exposed, with his undies and shorts glued to his ankles by a large pile of steamy webbing, which slowly poured out onto the ground as it started to hardened. He was thankful the safety vest was long enough to hide his unmentionables.

"Oh, that's no good," said Ian, squatting down to use extra hands to break up the nearly transparent mass from his underwear and shorts. "What good is that going to be? 'Excuse me, mister criminal, while I use my incredible spider powers,' and then I drop my shorts!"

Alex wasn't being helpful. "Freeze criminal, or I'll moon you!"

CHAPTER

17

Operation Filing Cabinet

It was Friday, and like most towns in the United Kingdom, people in Rossolington were thinking less about work and more about the weekend. Two precious days to enjoy the fruits of their labours, abuse their livers, and tell their alarm clocks what they could go do with themselves. A switching of mental gears that usually starts after lunch on Friday and doesn't properly switch back until Monday afternoon.

Mike Ridley couldn't switch gears, and he just ate lunch. He had made a deal with "The Brock" in exchange for a bonus that would create a two-week vacation in some fruity sounding French town (nice or niece or something), and an as yet unconfirmed period of marital bliss. To get there though, meant scouring the web for any and all safety themed training conferences he could send Frank to, and pushing his luck, a lot.

When the government's safety officer orders a seam closed, it's not because he feels like giving miners a break from their income. Frank wasn't a busybody looking to justify his hours at the pit with needless regulation. He genuinely cared about the miners, and the pit's perfect safety record was clear evidence that his no-fuss attitude in this regard had paid off. Since he'd been assigned to the Rossolington colliery there had been no fatalities. No more accidentally shattered families.

Mike hoped he would get most of the quota filled before Frank got back in a week's time, and have all the support equipment in place. No harm no foul. Except he knew Frank would want to inspect the supports himself before signing off on the dig, and the jig, as they say, would well and truly be up. He'll see the extra rooms dug out at the wrong ratio and freak out.

Mike tried to focus on the image of his wife. There were two versions. One carrying a rolling pin and a scowl, the other offering a beer and a smile. He also tried to recall all the supportive comments he had received when he announced they were going to mine the new seam, and the reassuring pat on the back from Mr. Brock. None of it was helping him justify betraying his friend and potentially putting his crew in danger. He knew full well Frank had everyone's best interests at heart, and his decision to close the seam until they could make it safe was just common sense. *Niece had better be nice*, thought Mike.

Alex and Ian decided to meet at their secret lair to get geared up for their mission to the pit. Their plan was simple. They would approach the mine from the woods to avoid detection, and then use ant and spider powers to find, climb, and enter Donald Brock's penthouse office suite. Once in, they would gather as much paperwork as they could find, bundle it up somehow, and then transport it back to their base of operations.

"You be the spider," said Ian.

"I don't want to be the spider. It's my mission so I'm going to be the ant."

As the sun set on Rossolington, the two boys turned on their torches and marched through the woods in single file along the hiking trail that circled the village. Both were fully decked out in their superhero garb. If anyone asked, they would say they were playing superhero—they were twelve-year-olds after all.

"Anyway, we only have one more spider capsule and it's in your utility belt," said Alex smiling. "Just don't think about webs."

"Very funny," grumbled Ian. "What was your other mission plan after we've robbed your dad's boss?"

"Oh yeah. I think you'll like this."

Alex, who was leading their little party, stopped and turned to face Ian.

"I was thinking about Rossolington. It doesn't really have a crime problem, does it?"

"Not really."

"Right. It does though, have a bully problem."

Ian smiled. "Yes, right. That's true. Look what you did to Darren, and there's the group that cut my knee that time. We could teach them all a lesson!"

"Absolutely," said Alex, and the boys resumed their walk through the woods. "I want to talk to Darren again. I bet he knows a few bullies. Maybe in other schools. We could really clean up the village."

From the trail, the two boys could see the backyard of the pit, an infrequently visited part of the colliery used to store old non-functioning mining tools. A graveyard for broken down Constant Miners and other equipment deemed past their useful date, old and rusty now after being fed to the humid temperate English climate. It was lit up by several bright flood lights, casting eerie shadows against the overgrown grass poking through gaps in the concrete slab ground.

"How are we going to get to the building without being seen? We don't have any flies." asked Ian.

Alex pondered for a moment; he hadn't factored the size of the yard in his plans. After a short think, he carefully pulled one of his matchbox drawers open with one hand as the other covered any possible escape route for the bug inside. "Time for some grasshopper power."

As the drawer opened, the grasshopper inside tried to leap away but was no match for Alex's quick reflexes. It was cupped in his covering hand mid-hop, safely contained and undamaged.

Alex grabbed his bottle of water, and quickly slapped his grasshopper holding hand against his wide open mouth, forcing the poor insect to the back of his throat before quickly washing it down with a large mouthful of water.

The transformation only took a few seconds.

First, the incredibly long antennae gracefully slid out of his forehead and then his eyes became bigger, brown and glossy. Alex was now super tuned in to his surroundings. Wind speed, nearby bug activity, he could sense it all. Alex could hear confused moths complain as they mindlessly bashed their heads against the floodlights in the yard, and he could feel rumblings underground as miners working the late shift dug for coal.

Alex's upper body started to shrink, as his two legs got longer and thicker. He was glad he decided to keep their school shorts as part of their superhero costume. Trousers would have surely been torn apart by now and that's something he'd have a hard time explaining to his mum.

Next, two extra arms emerged from either side of Alex's torso. He was now "boy-hopper" and ready to move. "We're going to jump past the lights. Get on my back."

"You're going to carry me?" asked Ian.

"Yeah sure, why not?"

"Because we didn't test that."

Ian reached into his pocket and pulled out his superpowers notebook. "Do you think you'll make it? According to my notes here, you'll barely make over there by yourself, never mind with me as a passenger. Why don't I eat a grasshopper and hop with you?"

"No, you need to change once we get there. I doubt I'll be able to force Brock's office window open with these puny grasshopper arms."

Alex turned his back to Ian. "All aboard."

"Fine, but I get to be the ant. I'll need all the strength I can get."

"Okay, you can be the ant."

Ian climbed onto Alex's back and held on tightly. Alex used his upper and lower set of arms to help hold Ian in place. Then, clumsily, used his long legs to step out of the woods and walk up to the tall perimeter fence surrounding the colliery.

Squatting down, Alex focused all his strength on his legs as he wound up for the jump. He could feel the power in them, like tightly coiled springs ready to explode. In their tests they had covered huge distances with each hop, but with the extra weight, Alex did wonder if Ian was right. He needed to clear the fence, and travel at least fifty feet across the yard in order to make it to the walkway directly behind the flood lights. "Ready Ian?"

"No."

Alex jumped and the two boys took off like a rocket, easily clearing the perimeter fence and its barbed wire coils. Ian tightened his grip as Alex looked down on the yard below them. Alex started to smile. *We're doing it, really doing it; the superhero game*, thought Alex. Putting their new abilities to good use just like in all their favourite comic books and movies. With the air rushing through Alex's "bowl-cut" hair, this mission felt exciting and dangerous. Even more so now as Alex noticed they were not going to make the walkway as hoped, but instead land about twenty feet short of their target, close to a large Constant Miner.

"We're not going to make it! We'll be seen!" shouted Ian.

"We'll have to jump again as soon as we land. We'll only be in the light for a second."

The boys started to descend, and Alex extended his long legs. He did this in part to control their fall but also to get ready to absorb the impact of their landing. In their tests, they learned the hard way how to land properly, and in the end, Ian's research into how paratroopers and parkour experts control their landings really came in handy after several experimental leaps ended painfully.

"Here we go!" shouted Alex. The ground came up fast, and Alex transferred the energy of their falling weight into his powerful legs as they hit the concrete. He then leaned forward and pushed the energy back into the ground, shooting the two boys off like a rocket once again. Having been barely exposed to the flood lights glare, Alex quickly pondered what the security footage would look like: Two kids dressed in orange safety vests and dust masks, piggybacked and leaping through the frame in less than a second. He wondered if his dad would bring home the security tape. It would be cool to see themselves in action on the telly.

The second leap turned out to be much more powerful than the first and the boys flew past their intended target, landing on the colliery roof, handily just meters from what they suspected was Donald Brock's office, the tallest and newest looking part of the building and custom work space for his royal bossiness. Ian climbed off Alex's back, and the two boys carefully crawled over to the window looking into Brock's office. Alex used his large compound eyes and antennae to scan the dark room inside.

"This has to be it. Everything inside looks and smells expensive," said Alex.

"Right," confirmed Ian. "What now?"

"Well, you need to change into an ant and get that window open. Remember, don't break the glass. I'll need a few minutes for my grasshopper powers to wear off."

"Okey dokey," said Ian, and remembering the aftereffects of the grasshopper experiments they did before, he moved a few feet away from Alex.

"Where are you going?"

"Any minute now you're going to fart. It'll sound like boiling sewage, and smell even worse, so I'll just be over here at a safe distance. Okay?"

Alex shrugged and then nodded. He had to agree with his friend's assessment. The only bad part of this amazing superhero adventure were the aftereffects. Bad stomach pain and smelly farts. *It's not fair*, thought Alex. It's not like Spider-Man had to deal with this kind of thing.

CHAPTER 18

Boldly Going Secti

The Nest was abuzz! Word of a long forgotten research mission suddenly becoming active and sending back samples travelled quickly. A new world inhabited by creatures very similar to their own flesh and hard shell ancestors was huge news. Heading up the first research mission to this new distant planet, was a very proud Administrator Reddish Brown.

Over the last few days, more samples had arrived from the new planet. The most recent being another one of those hilarious hopping creatures, considered an evolutionary joke to the Secti. *I mean really, hopping, so funny, what an awkward way to travel. You leap without any clue as to where you'll land? Craziness.*

Another new addition was also introduced to the fast growing zoo of aliens, an eight-legged creature their other alien guests were not happy to see. The carnivorous beast had to be quarantined soon after it arrived because it kept trying to trap and kill everyone. Several Secti had blindly wandered into the strange creature's webbing and found themselves quickly wrapped and chewed upon until the silly little thing realized they weren't edible. A fascinating experience, by all accounts.

There was even chemical chatter about setting up a special "victim theme park" for Secti interested in the sensation.

Reddish Brown had assembled a team to explore the new world and they were lined up for the entire Nest to celebrate. They were sporting the latest in battle ready robotic engineering, similar in design to their workaday robot form; big head, six appendages and stubby antennae, but twice the size and reinforced with much stronger motors and linkages. They were a little slower than their usual rides but designed to take a beating. Something the Secti considered a prudent precaution after learning about the brutal Inside-Outs reign of terror on their visitor's home world.

"First we have Marketing Magician Maroon," emitted Reddish Brown to the receptors transmitting his chemical signal to the Nest. "In charge of assessing the Inside-Out threat and properly communicating our response."

Emitters in the control panel squirted a rainbow of approval. Reddish Brown continued with this presentation.

"Visionary Officer Blueish will be in charge of our future plans for this new world."

Blueish took a bow as Reddish Brown continued.

"In charge of being our muse on this adventure is Thought Provoker Red. A Nest veteran, descended from the first Secti that transitioned from their biological forms millions of Nest cycles ago. We're very lucky to have Red with us today."

Red waved a limb regally and the emitters once again signalled their approval.

"And finally, our Secti in charge of rash reactions and attack, Instigation Officer Infected Yellow. Making sure we don't overlook the bizarre and instructed to select the most random responses. A real out-of-the-confined-space thinker, this one."

Infected Yellow coolly tapped his large head a couple of times, letting Secti watching the presentation know they could trust the insanity waiting inside.

The Secti, as an ancient (by human measurements) race, had pretty much done it all. Poverty, wars, disease, plagues, greed. At one point or another during the billions of years the Secti had been evolving, they had tried every social model they could think of. It wasn't until they discovered how to transfer their conscious minds into machines that they finally found peace.

Unbound by the limitations of flesh and shell bodies—and the constant need to stuff food into them—they were free. A trip to another part of the Nest was easy. A Secti would just upload to the network and send themselves to an available robot host anywhere on the planet in seconds.

This also opened up new markets for robot design. If a Secti wanted a climb up the Great Mound, there was no physical preparation needed. Just an upload to the latest and greatest body designed for that task and off they went. Nothing was impossible: flying, swimming, combat. There was a robot body ready for each and every activity the Secti could dream of, and without the need for flesh and blood bodies, all of their old-world problems disappeared quickly. No more fighting over land and resources. No more forgotten poor. The appeal of wealth and power over others disappeared as new intellectual frontiers were created. When the Secti were no longer worried about where their next meal was coming from, they had a lot more time to be constructive and creative.

The final hurdle the Secti had to overcome as an evolving species was to combat the boredom. Peace and tranquillity were all well and good, but also incredibly dull. Secti, awash with gracious platitudes and intellectual conversation, quickly tired of the serenity, so a small number of new roles were created to mix things up. Instigation Officers would travel the Nest and perform random acts. They would make a nuisance of themselves and even pick fights with other Secti. Anything they could to disrupt the status quo and liven up an otherwise mundane productive day.

Other job titles followed and before anyone cared to notice, the planet was inundated in Visionary Officers, Marketing Magicians and Client Success Directors. Colourful titles that had little to no connection to their actual tasks, but looked good when a Secti introduced itself.

The Secti had developed the perfect society by realizing there was no such thing. Administrator Reddish Brown, however, thought there was more they could do to correctly screw up their utopia. One last ingredient for their societal soup to give it that tiniest hint of a bad aftertaste. Still enjoyable, but not so good to stop trying to improve it. This social engineering project had become a personal obsession for Reddish.

Once balance and peace had almost been achieved at home, the Secti looked towards the stars. Using their newfound ability to network and share ideas with a planet-sized network of talent, they soon developed a method to explore the universe around them.

The Nest sat in a remote section of one of the Milky Way's spiral arms and was, in fact, the only planet in their solar system. It didn't even have a moon. The nearest planets were light years away, so rather than build rockets powerful enough to escape the Nest's huge gravitational pull, they developed portal technology, a system that bends space time to open small wormholes between two locations anywhere in the galaxy. There was just one problem. They needed a portal platform at each end of the wormhole for it to be stable enough to use.

One day, an idea started to bounce around the Secti network. That of the creation of tiny nanobots that could be more easily catapulted out into the galaxy and programmed to find a suitable power source. Then using their own tiny bodies, they would convert their surroundings into the portal that would connect with the Nest and send back samples. Simple, brilliant, and a lot easier than blasting Secti off in rockets. This also meant Secti didn't have to leave the Nest and separate themselves from the network, which was a really unsettling thing to do after they had gotten used to being a collective.

Client Success Director Orangey-Blue waved to get Reddish Brown's attention. "Administrator, two more visitors coming through the portal."

Reddish Brown gestured for his team to step off the transport pad to make room for their newest guests, and after a double flash of light, pop pop, an ant and a spider appeared on the platform.

"Quick, get them separated!" instructed Reddish Brown.

A team of Secti ran towards the confused creatures. The ant, concerned about the location of its queen, frantically scanned for any chemical word about its creator. The spider, on the other hand, on seeing the approaching Secti, took a more aggressive stance and struggled against the planet's stronger gravitation pull to raise its front two legs as a show of force.

The Secti, having learned quickly after their first encounter with this species, surrounded the spider and grabbed its legs, safely rendering it harmless as they lifted and transported the angry arachnid to his new garden home. The ant was easier to deal with; it only took one Secti to coax the insect off the pad with the promise[13] that its queen awaited it in another part of the city. Once cleared, Reddish Brown stepped onto the transport pad and gestured for his team to join him. He addressed the Secti watching and sampling the presentation around the Nest.

"Today, we Secti take a bold step. Perhaps into our own past, but also a journey likely filled with fantastic new discoveries. We are honoured to represent the Secti race as we broaden our understanding of the galaxy. We are ready. Ready to show the universe what the Secti are made of, the great advances we've made, and the social order we have achieved together. We shall evaluate this Inside-Out menace, and pass judgement on their cruel treatment of our ancestors. Farewell."

Reddish Brown signalled to Orangey-Blue. "Time to go."

---

[13] Lie.

CHAPTER 19

Clever Vomit

Alex threw up.

This wasn't your standard, pea soup variety of stomach ejection, or even the more disgusting egg-white consistency type of eruption frequently mixed with corn (whether you'd eaten any or not). This wasn't a full-on evacuation of Alex's innards or one of those fake looking vomitus moments you see in movies where the actor spits out clam chowder.

This intestinal rewind was like nothing Alex had ever experienced before. There was no stomach pain or wooziness, just the feeling that something deep within Alex wanted to get out and explore. Upchuck with a game plan, slowly climbing up through his oesophagus and throat, and then onto the back of Alex's tongue, which forced him to cough and eject the clever sputum onto Donald Brock's expensive-looking desk.

Vomit, however, doesn't usually do triple summersaults before nailing its landing, or look like five tiny robots. And puke doesn't (as far as Alex and Ian knew) declare it's from a distant planet and demand your unconditional surrender.

"I'm not hearing anything. How am I understanding what these little robots are saying?" asked Alex.

"That's what you're worried about? You just coughed up robots!" said Ian.

"Well sure, but right now I also have six arms and can shoot webs out of my bum, so compared to the other strange things that have happened recently, this doesn't seem that weird."

One of the tiny robots stepped forward and his antennae started to wiggle. "Take me to your leader."

"Maybe they're like the insects. Every time we change we pick up chatter from the bugs through our antennae. Maybe they're some kind of super robot insect. They do have six legs," said Ian.

Alex leaned in closer, and used one of his larger spider eyes to get a better look at their new visitors. "Wow, these little guys are cool, take a look."

From the shiny white armour and black joints to the bulbous heads and large glowing eyes, these little machines, barely a centimetre tall, were strangely beautiful—sleek, practical and graceful. The other four robots had spread out and were leaping around the office, examining the furniture, books and paintings. The one standing in front of Alex and Ian folded four of its arms and tapped his foot impatiently.

"I think this one is getting irritated with us," said Ian.

"How can you tell?"

"He's starting to look like my dad."

Alex for no logical reason, started to shout at the tiny robot. "Are—you—mad—at—us? What—is—your—name?"

"Why are you talking like that?" asked Ian. "I doubt he's deaf."

"How do you know? I don't see any ears, or a mouth, just tiny antennae and those big light brown eyes."

The tiny robot stepped forward. "That's almost my name."

"What? Eyes?" asked Alex.

"Don't be silly. My name is Reddish Brown."

Ian and Alex exchanged a puzzled glance.

"What kind of name is that?" asked Ian.

"Mine," said Reddish Brown.

The other Secti, after finishing their tour of the office, leapt back onto the desk to re-join Reddish. Infected Yellow took a route past Ian's head to give it an experimental kick before re-joining the group.

"Ouch!" Ian complained.

"These are the members of my team: Marketing Magician Maroon, Visionary Officer Blueish, Thought Provoker Red, and Instigation Officer Infected Yellow."

Alex and Ian leaned in again to get a better look at Infected Yellow's eyes, and nodded in agreement. They were indeed the colour of pus.

Prior to the robots' arrival, the boys were making good progress with their plan to steal Donald Brock's paperwork. Ian, not content to use his mega-ant powers to simply force open the window to the office, decided to remove it completely, frame and all. His zeal to demonstrate his awesome strength wasn't limited to construction projects either, and once the boys were inside Donald's office, he gleefully pulled one of the larger filing cabinets from the wall to use as storage for all the other papers they could find.

If it had text, written or printed, it went in the cabinet and, once full, was wrapped in webbing. Well, once it was full and Ian agreed to turn away while Alex dropped his shorts to use his less than convenient spider powers, it was wrapped with webbing.

Then Alex threw up tiny robots, and what historians might eventually call the most monumental event in human history, happened while the boys were committing industrial espionage, and Alex's shorts were keeping his ankle's warm.

Alex pulled up his shorts. "My name is Alex, and this is Ian."

"What strange names. How do they describe you? Is there something especially Ian or Alex about you?" asked Marketing Magician Maroon.

"Describe us? They're names," said Ian.

"And that's it? They're just labels?" asked Thought Provoker Red.

"Well, Alex is short for Alexander, but yeah, they're just names," said Alex.

Suddenly, Ian's wrist-watch started to beep. "Damn, we're about to change back."

The boys stepped away from Donald's desk and gave each other a little space. Ian's transformation started before Alex's.

First came the pins and needles and intense stomach pain, followed by a massive fart! It was a sound akin to a fireworks celebration combined with the noise you'd expect from bag pipes filled with wet cement. A horrible sound followed by an even worse smell, and Ian groaned as he waved his original hands in front of his nose while his skin and eyes returned to normal, and his extra limbs and antennae were absorbed back into his body.

Alex took another step away from Ian and the stink, then felt his transformation begin. Being that his spider was on the smaller side, the more explosive elements of his transformation were less violent, resulting in a fart that sounded like a dying trumpet followed by a smell similar to rotting cabbage. His extra eyes were sucked back into his forehead and vanished, and his spare arms were quickly pulled back into his body.

Reddish Brown and his team looked on, antennae wiggling.

"Wait, are these little robots saying anything?" asked Ian. "I see their antennae moving but I'm not picking anything up now."

"Neither am I," said Alex.

"I don't think they're picking up our chemical message now that the nanobots have finished processing the aliens they consumed," said Reddish Brown.

"I concur," said Visionary Officer Blueish. "I wasn't aware the nanobots were designed for this kind of thing. The side effects of the transportation process are quite remarkable."

Satisfied Alex and Ian couldn't read them anymore, the group turned to face each other.

"Well, the nanobots were supposed to find a renewable power source and build a portal, which is what they've done. I'm not sure how they ended up inside these Inside-Outs, but the plan does seem to be working. We're getting samples after all," said Reddish Brown.

"I say we hurt one of them. Establish our superiority," said Infected Yellow.

"No, that wouldn't be a useful random action right now, Yellow," said Thought Provoker Red. "We currently have two portals back to the Nest we can use. We've also met the only, I surmise, two Inside-Outs we can communicate with. View the second Inside-Out as a spare in case we break one."

Reddish Brown suddenly fell forward as Alex tapped his back. "Hey—we—can't—hear—you!"

As Reddish Brown got to his feet, he became aware of another large lifeform closing in on their location. "Wait, do you sense that?"

Infected Yellow turned towards the large double-doors on the far side of the room. "Yes, another lifeform is approaching. Much larger than the ones here. Shall I engage?"

"No," said Reddish Brown, "we should try to minimize our exposure until we have a better understanding of this planet."

Alex and Ian were confused. First the tiny robots seemed to be having a meeting, and then they faced the boys and pointed at the double doors leading to Donald's office.

"I think someone is coming," said Ian.

"I don't hear anything. Maybe they want to leave."

Alex and Ian then heard the jangling of keys in the next room.

"Bollocks! Someone's coming," said Alex. "Quick, we need to transform and get out of here with the files!"

Alex and Ian reached for their utility belts.

"What are we changing into?" asked Ian.

"Same thing that got us here. You be an ant again and I'll hop us back to the woods."

The Secti studied both boys as they consumed the helpless creatures they had held captive inside the containers strapped to their bodies.

"Fascinating," said Marketing Magician Maroon. "Our nanobots have a complete lock on those Inside-Out forms, right down to the cellular level."

"The transformation is surprisingly quick," said Reddish Brown.

Ian effortlessly picked up the large filing cabinet and pushed it through the opening in the wall where the window used to be. He and Alex then climbed out of the office onto the roof.

"They appear to be leaving. Perhaps they also don't want to be discovered by the larger Inside-Out," said Blueish.

"We should follow and investigate further. We don't want to lose sight of our only way back to the Nest," said Reddish Brown.

The five Secti took aim at the opening in the wall and quickly jumped through it. Since the Earth was so much smaller than the Nest, the gravitational pull was no match for their tougher battle-ready bodies. Instigation Officer Infected Yellow calculated in their current form, they were easily as strong as the Inside-Outs they had scanned so far, and if it came to a fight, these fleshy creatures wouldn't stand a chance against a Secti invasion.

Ian picked up the window he had uninstalled earlier and quickly forced it back into the opening in the wall. He then picked up the filing cabinet and joined Alex, who was gearing up for the jump near the roof edge.

"This isn't going to be easy," said Alex as he looked out past the security lights and courtyard below. "It's going to take a few hops to make it back. We'll be caught on the security cameras for sure."

"I don't think we have much choice. At least all they'll see is our backs, right? It's not like we're one hundred percent ourselves at the moment," said Ian.

"Good point. Okay, you grab hold of the cabinet, I'll grab hold of you."

Alex leaped, but with the extra weight of the cabinet the boys only travelled twenty feet, just enough to clear the roof and the walkway located right behind the security lights. The second leap got them closer to the perimeter fence, but because Alex couldn't see much past Ian and the cabinet, they jumped more to the side. Alex tried to correct this with his next leap, but the extra weight caused the group to land awkwardly. The next jump sent them backwards and they crashed into an old Constant Miner. Alex and Ian pushed up against the machine to shield themselves from the security lights.

"You okay?" asked Ian.

"Yeah. It's hard to move in the right direction. Come on, we've got to get out of here."

Alex wound himself up for the jump. Blast off!

This time they headed in the right direction and managed to cover another twenty-five feet, which put them within hoping distance of the woods. They just had to clear the perimeter fence and barbed wire. Alex wanted to get this right, so rather than attempt to channel the momentum from the last jump, he landed and carefully pointed the group at the woods to make sure it counted. The delay exposed them longer than they would have liked, but Alex didn't care at this point. He just wanted to get back into the woods and their secret lair.

The last jump saw the two boys clear the yard and head straight into the trees, crashing through thick branches to eventually fall to the ground. Anyone within a mile would have probably heard the commotion.

Alex and Ian lay there for a moment, breathing hard. Their enhanced bodies were uninjured by the fall, but their vests were badly damaged. The exposed sides of their safety vests were great for their transformations, but also easily hooked and torn by the trees. The cabinet on the other hand, remained intact thanks to its web covering.

"Okay, we're never doing anything like that again," said Alex.

Ian got to his feet and dusted himself off. "We should get this cabinet back to base."

"Absolutely," said Alex. "Hey, I wonder what happened to those little robots."

Reddish Brown and his team leaped through the air and landed on Alex's chest.

"Oh, there you are," said Alex. "I have a question."

"Yes?" asked Reddish Brown.

"What's a nanobot?"

CHAPTER 20

Video and Radio

Donald Brock collapsed into his Nappa leather chair, took his glasses off and rubbed his face. All he wanted to do was smoke his cigar, drink some brandy, and get some peace and quiet away from the mansion and his wife's latest *experiment* in the kitchen. *Was that too much to ask?*

What Donald got instead was acid reflux and a mystery to investigate. A how, why, who, and where to solve in regards to his filing cabinet and every single scrap of paper in his office.

The "why" probably had something to do with certain extra dealings he'd made with some third parties, a private sale he had arranged for the extra coal he was extracting from each seam in the mine. The people who knew anything about that deal, however, only stood to benefit from the arrangement, so why stab him in the back? Blackmail, maybe? Take the extra coal, and then avoid payment by threatening to report Donald to the police? Plausible, but stupid since he wouldn't be taken down alone. As theories went, though, it was the best he could come up with at present, and it did also help answer the "who" part of this mystery.

Donald figured out the "how" pretty easily, it was just difficult to believe. The burglars must have taken his filing cabinet out through the window. He could tell because when he went to open it, he discovered the latch was upside down, in fact, the entire window was upside down. The crooks had somehow plucked it out of the wall, and then reinstalled it incorrectly. *Easily a job for four or five men*, thought Donald. They'd need that many to lift and push the heavy cabinet out of the window, and then carry it across the roof and beyond the colliery. Donald grabbed his keys and unlocked an armoire behind his desk. Inside the armoire were two small monitors displaying various views around the mine and a stack of recording equipment. One monitor exclusively displayed images of the yard behind the pit, and the miners parking lot. The second monitor displayed an image of his secretary's desk and the main office floor below.

Alex and Ian collapsed onto their sofa. What had started out as a cool superhero adventure had suddenly gotten very technical and a bit icky. There were billions of tiny robots crawling through their bodies, changing and fixing things and transporting the bugs they were eating to a planet called the Nest.

That pins and needles feeling suddenly had a creepy visual to go with it: a miniscule, insect-like robot with spindly pointy legs, and a single glowing red eye, creepily scurrying over their cells and floating through their veins. They were machines that could manipulate bones and proteins as they created a matrix around the boy's live insect snacks before transporting them to the Secti's home world. The process was like a photocopy projected outward through their bodies, adapting human and insect bodies to temporarily produce a creature that combined the best of both.

The boys felt foolish. They'd not even considered how this was all happening, or the implications. They'd just loved how it made them feel and what it could do for them. In their little world filled with bullies trying to beat them up, it was intoxicating to suddenly feel powerful and actually be in control of their destinies for once.

Alex and Ian stared in disbelief at Administrator Reddish Brown as he laid it out for them. The Secti, the portal technology, the nanobots. They were glad when their powers wore off and they were no longer able to understand what Reddish was saying. Now they just sat and bathed in the odours following the intestinal backfire that signalled their return to normal. Not that they were normal anymore.

"So now what?" asked Ian.

"I don't know," said Alex. "You heard Reddish Brown. The nanobots are there for good maintaining that portal thingy, and these Secti want us to keep sending samples."

Donald watched the recording for an eleventh time. There they were, two boys (he guessed) dressed like an ant and a grasshopper, but wearing safety gear, hopping over the perimeter fence. Then, about twenty minutes later, they hopped away from the mine with his filing cabinet. Leaping around the yard for a bit, they eventually disappeared into the woods.

This had to be a joke or something, thought Donald. A prank surely. *One of those faked videos you see online all the time.* If that was the case, Donald had to admit the visual effects were amazing. In a few days his business partners would drive up with their payment and the cabinet laughing their asses off. They'd show him how it was all arranged as they celebrated over cocktails when Donald's new quotas were filled. Donald started the video one more time.

Satisfied the robbery was some kind of practical joke, Donald poured himself a brandy and smiled. *What a great trick*, he thought. He knew his clients were well connected but he wasn't expecting anything like this. He sank into his comfortable chair and took a sip of his drink. He then pulled out a fresh new cigar from his jacket pocket and unwrapped it. A clip and a light followed, then a sweet, satisfying cloud of smoke billowed from his mouth.

"So what do we do now?" asked Ian.

"Not sure. Keep calm and just carry on eating bugs, I guess," said Alex. "It's not like we can do anything about the nanobots, and it's not like anything bad has happened. If anything, everything's gotten better."

"Fair point."

"I still want to teach Rossolington's bullies a lesson, that's for sure."

The boys became aware of a rustling sound coming from one of their many boxes of junk stored in their lair. Then, from out of the hodgepodge of old computer equipment, television parts, and other assorted electronic components emerged a small, old and broken transistor radio. Its volume control was missing and the back was completely removed—one of the many victims of the boy's curiosity over the years. Someone's out of date tech, ripped apart to see how it ticked, but never successfully put together again.

With Reddish Brown's help, the radio hopped onto the dressing table, closely followed by the other members of the Secti group, each carrying a battery.

The radio's long antenna was removed, and each of the four batteries got a blast of power from the Secti holding them. A very brief flicker of their eyes signalled the transfer of power before the batteries were placed inside the radio. The team of robots then walked around the back of the device and got to work on its electronic components, quickly figuring out its circuitry, and making the necessary repairs to make it work again. In just a couple of minutes, the radio was brought back to life and a local South Yorkshire radio talk show conversation about homing pigeons could be heard.

A short while later, all of them, except Reddish Brown, reached up and removed their antennae. They handed them to Reddish, who connected them together to produce two larger antennae, and then Reddish connected them to the top of the radio through two small holes the group had made earlier.

"Testing, testing. Inside-Outs, sorry, I mean humans. Do you hear me?"

The voice, which the boys assumed was Reddish Brown's, quietly squeaked out of the radio's single speaker. It was a voice like something you'd expect from one of Snow White's mates, high on helium. The boys giggled.

"I can assume from the silly noises you're making that you can hear me just fine," said Reddish Brown sounding a little irritated. "May I remind you we Secti have travelled 120 light years and just adapted your childish alien technology to convert chemical-based communication into soundwaves. We also learned your language in less than an hour."

Alex and Ian managed to compose themselves for a moment. "Yes, we can hear you."

"Can you say, follow the yellow brick road, follow the yellow brick road?" asked Ian.

Alex and Ian started laughing out loud and Reddish Brown's eyes glowed a little more intensely. "No."

After a few seconds, the boys wiped the tears from their eyes and took a deep breath.

"We're sorry. We couldn't help it," said Alex.

"Clearly," said Reddish Brown. "Impulse control doesn't appear to be one of your race's strengths."

Reddish Brown jumped up on top of the small radio. "Now if you two could just focus for a moment, I have something to discuss with you."

Alex and Ian shuffled forward and leaned in closer.

"First of all, my team, who have generously donated their antennae and power so that I can communicate with you on your level, need to travel back to the Nest. Secondly, I will remain behind to further study your world and catalogue its many insect species."

The boys exchanged a glance.

"Err, how do they get back?" asked Ian.

"The same way they arrived," said Reddish Brown.

CHAPTER 21

Bully the Bully

The next Monday at school, Alex and Ian received a tip from a kid, who knew a kid, who was friends with someone Darren was planning to beat up after school. Robin Bank's erstwhile bully it seemed, had fully recovered from his first encounter with Alex the human ladybird and had resumed his favourite hobby: picking on people smaller than himself.

The information they received put the meeting behind the school's bike sheds after everyone had gone home. It was a perfect place to question the school's top bully and hopefully learn more about Rossolington's network of tormentors. Assuming, of course, these people kept tabs on one another. How else would they be able to tell the difference between a fellow bully and the bullied? Did bullies bully other bullies? Perhaps they were all part of a gang and maybe they had monthly meetings or a secret handshake. Alex and Ian were looking forward to finding out.

Darren's future victim, the acquaintance acquaintance's friend, was told to skip the beating with the promise that Darren would be "taken care of."

The meeting was set for 6 p.m. So after tea, Alex and Ian met up at their lair to get ready for the mission. Administrator Reddish Brown was waiting for them.

"You're going to do what now?" asked Reddish, his munchkin voice broadcasted from the small transistor radio.

"We're going to take on our school's worst bully," said Alex.

"And make him tell us about all the other bullies he knows about. We're making a list," said Ian.

"Interesting," said Reddish Brown. "And you're going to use the Secti-nanobots to transform into something that will give you the upper hand in the conflict. Turn into superheroes, as you put it."

Alex and Ian unpacked their dust masks and the new vests Alex had "borrowed" from his father's stash of safety equipment.

"That's right. I'm thinking flies tonight." Alex smiled.

Ian tapped one of his utility belt's medicine bottles and grinned. "I finally managed to grab some more. They're really hard to capture intact."

"And even harder to eat without their wings coming off," said Alex.

Alex took a moment to wonder how his wingless test fly was doing on the Secti home world.

"Not to worry," said Ian. "I figure all we have to do is pour a little water into the bottles first. Get the flies wet. They won't be able to move about as much and it won't hurt them. They'll be easier to swallow that way, too. Red, will your people be okay with that?"

"Actually, having those particular creatures a little subdued when they get to the Nest would be helpful. We'd have time to get them situated before we dry them off and let them go about their business. They're quite the roguish characters. We've often thought about introducing them to the spiders."

Alex and Ian smiled. They had only known the tiny robot for a few days but were surprised that such a super sophisticated alien would crack a joke like that.

Administrator Reddish Brown had had quite the day in Rossolington while the boys were at school. He started the day with a nice early morning charge under the Earth's power dense yellow sun, and then continued his research mission, starting with the massive vegetation (relative to a Secti) and local insect population.

This resulted in a series of interesting encounters with everything from queen ants to honey bees and butterflies. They were mostly drama free when dealing with his vegetarian ancestors but occasionally combative as he approached the more carnivorous of Earth's insect population. Reddish was glad his team chose to travel to Earth in their battle-ready gear and was happy to let earwigs, spiders, and even ants try their attacks, if only to study how the different creatures went about obtaining fuel to survive. The information would be vital when the Secti got serious about creating an eco-system for these creatures back home.

The most impressive insect he found was a variation of the ladybird, only much bigger (twice as tall as Reddish in his current form) and less colourful. It sported massive mandibles up front. He recorded a holographic image to show his two human contacts. He was curious what name they had given this species and wondered if they'd be willing to send one to the Nest. A tall order, considering the bug's size versus the capacity of the mouths and throats leading back to his planet. *We'll have to send more nanobots to Earth and construct a larger portal,* thought Reddish. Maybe the humans would allow him to draw some nanobots from their blood and let them self-replicate using the raw materials in the boy's junk boxes. Reddish, however, had noted a certain skittishness the humans had about medical matters and even certain types of insects. Strange, considering their size and technological dominance over their planet. He chalked up their cowardly nature to immaturity.

The Earth, however, belonged to the humans. They had won the evolutionary race and had begun to enhance their lives with technology, as the Secti had done several million years ago. It was an uncomfortable reality the visiting Secti had had to accept when they arrived. They deplored the treatment of their ancestral cousins but had to recognize the natural order of things on this planet and not interfere. Instigation Officer Infected Yellow's invasion plans would have to be postponed, at least for now.

The planet's size and location within its solar system favoured the human species above others. They were, as his contact Ian described, in the "Goldilocks zone." The right size creatures on the right sized planet the right distance from its Sun. This planet's insect population didn't stand a chance with so many big creatures stomping about.

Reddish Brown already missed the Nest. It was the first time he'd operated solo, and he looked forward to completing his reconnaissance mission and reconnecting with the network. Until that glorious day came, he would put together a menu of insects for his new human contacts and record everything he saw. If they were going to grow and maintain their collection of insects in the Nest, they would need to provide more food options. The spiders would certainly appreciate something live to hunt and snack on, he was sure. A fully functioning, self-maintaining eco system would take time to create. A detailed study of insect behaviour might also inspire tweaks to the Secti social system and further perfect its imperfections.

At 5:50 p.m., Alex and Ian swallowed one fly each and transformed. An extra set of arms and a fine set of wings shot out from their bodies. Their eyes became much larger too, giving them a great multi-window view of their surroundings. Like a kaleidoscope image, but made to make sense as the nanobots combined the fly's central visual core with the boy's human optic nerves. They made the necessary visual cortex adjustments in the boys' brains to blend a fly's superior visual scope, with the human brain's ability to see most of the visual light spectrum.

The hairs on their arms got longer and tougher, and the two boys could feel the tiniest shifts in air pressure around them. With senses this acute, even a fully trained ninja wouldn't be able to sneak up on them. It was time to fly.

The boys took off and headed to the top of the trees. The sun was almost set and Rossolington's street lights were slowly blinking to life. From their position, they could see Robin Bank school and the top of Darren's house, and they were happy to note there were very few people out on the streets. Most were no doubt sprawled out on their sofa's at home in front of the telly after tea, rubbing satisfied bellies.

Their first stop was Darren's house to make sure he was actually following through with his appointment.

"Ready?" asked Alex.

"Ready," said Ian.

The boys pushed off from the trees and made a beeline (flyline?) for Darren's house. The trip took less than two seconds. They slowly hovered high above the house, exactly like two flies zeroing in on a rancid snack. Their improved ears listened for any movement from Darren's house. They didn't have to wait for long before Darren appeared.

Darren stumbled out of the back of the house and fell over. Another much larger figure appeared and stood over him, wielding a leather belt in one hand and holding a beer bottle in the other. *Must be Darren's dad,* thought Alex. He was a bulky man, still covered in coal dust after a day in the mine, his dirty white vest barely concealing his beer gut and chunky, hairy arms.

From their vantage point, the boys could hear the much larger man yelling at Darren, each word punctuated with another slap of his belt. "What. Did. I. Say?"

Darren seemed too afraid to respond.

"WELL?" The belt came down again and the buckle caught Darren's hand as he tried to shield his legs. Darren cried out in agony.

"Oh don't be such a baby! Man up. I don't work all day to support a cry-baby."

Cradling his hurt hand, Darren rolled over and got to his feet, tears streaming down his face.

"Stop bloody crying," yelled the man. "Get to the bloody store and get my cigs like I told you!"

The larger man turned and stomped back into the house and slammed the back-door. Darren hobbled to the end of the yard, opened the gate, and took off down the alleyway behind the houses towards Alexandra Road. Alex and Ian flew ahead to the bike sheds at Robin Back School to wait for him.

The boys arrived a few seconds later and attached themselves to the side of the building overlooking the bike sheds. A single security light lit the eerily deserted part of the school, which by day was the go-to location for fledgling couples looking for privacy, or bullies to conduct their business.

Ian turned to Alex. "So do you still want to go through with this?"

"Yeah, why wouldn't I?"

"I don't know, looks like Darren's already had enough today. Was that his dad? He's pretty mean."

"Yeah, just like Darren. Did you forget what he did to you the other day?"

"No, but I'm okay now."

"Yeah, because you're loaded with those little robots. If you didn't you'd probably be in the hospital. It's time Darren was taught a lesson."

"Ten-four to that," said Ian.

"Ten-four?"

"Yeah, that's what secret agents say when they understand something."

"Oh, okay, ten-four then."

"I just realized something." Ian smirked.

"What?"

"We're literally flies on the wall!"

The boys chuckled for a moment, but then a subtle change in the air flow around them suggested someone was coming.

Darren appeared below them, still cradling his hand as he walked back and forth looking for his arranged victim. Alex and Ian were sure Darren would get angry having been stood up, but instead he looked nervous and frustrated. He walked up to the school building and sat against the wall. Darren started to cry again.

"What are you crying about, bully?" shouted Alex.

Darren jumped to his feet and looked around but couldn't see where the voice came from.

"Up here, bully," shouted Ian.

Wings a blur, four arms, two legs, the boys descended on Darren. Making a monstrous buzzing noise as they got closer and closer. Darren tried to run, but his legs were still sore after his beating and not even fully recovered after Alex tossed him like a basketball a few days ago. He struggled to run into the open playground, but Ian cut off his escape. He turned to run in the opposite direction towards the teacher's parking lot, but was stopped by Alex. With the school building on the left and the bike sheds on the right, there was nowhere for Darren to go. The Bug Boys slowly closed in on their target, their wings still buzzing, blowing litter and leaves at Darren. Buffeting the bully back and forth and with no solution presenting itself, Darren fell to his knees and buried his face in his hands.

Abruptly, the buzzing stopped. Darren, shaking, slowly uncovered his face and saw the Bug Boys standing over him. Their big, emotionless compound eyes stared blankly at him. Their top set of arms were crossed and the second set positioned in full superhero mode, fists resting on their hips.

"Do you know who we are, Darren?" asked Alex.

Darren shook his head, terrified, tears streaming down his face.

"Grab his ears. That should jog his memory," said Alex.

Ian clamped his hands around Darren's ears and pushed his thumbnails against the cartilage inside, hard. Darren tried to scream, but Ian covered his mouth. The bully tried to pull Ian's hands away from his face, but the tough hairs on Ian's arm poked his hands.

"Remember us now? You used to like doing this to us. I thought we told you to stop bullying."

Darren nodded his head, and Ian uncovered his mouth.

"Alex? Ian?"

"That's the Bug Boys to you," said Ian. Deliberately trying to project his voice to sound as heroic as possible.

"Bug Boys?"

"That's right, Darren, Rossolington's newest superheroes, and we're here to put an end to your bullying," said Alex.

"Really? Please don't," pleaded Darren.

Alex and Ian did a double-take. They weren't expecting any push back at this point in the mission. Darren was clearly beaten, and not even by them really, so it was surprising he would beg to protect his side business of extorting money out of kids at the school.

"What do you mean, 'please don't?' Stop bullying, that's an order," said Ian, who pressed his fingernails against Darren's ears a little harder to make his point.

Darren shuffled forward a couple of inches on his knees and cupped his hands together to plead his case. "I need the money. My mum moved out a couple of months ago. She couldn't take it anymore. Living with my dad, that is. I need the cash for train tickets. You see this?"

Darren held out his dirty hand and the boys saw a deep cut bleeding out. It was likely caused by his father's belt buckle. "That's what he did to me today, and that's not the worst of it."

Ian let go of Darren's ears and reached for his utility belt. He opened a match box with a red cross drawn on it, and pulled out a large Band-Aid. Ian then unpacked the plaster, took Darren's hand and covered the cut.

"So why haven't you called the police or something?" asked Ian.

"Are you crazy? If they didn't believe me it would only make things worse at home, and I have to watch out for my little sister too. Mum tried to take us with her, but my dad stopped her."

Why do things always get complicated? thought Alex. This was supposed to be simple—get the bully to stop terrorizing kids at school. Now there were layers, and Alex couldn't believe he was actually feeling sorry for Darren Wilkins. His super nanobot enhanced brain, however, had a light-bulb moment.

"So how much more money do you need?" asked Alex.

"Only twenty more pounds to go and I can afford a ticket for me and my sis," said Darren.

"Okay, so how about this. We've still got the fifteen pounds we raised for you and should be able to scrounge up another five. If we give you the twenty, you'll have enough to go be with your mum and the bullying can stop. Right?"

Darren wiped his eyes and smiled. "Yes, absolutely! There's a train leaving tomorrow night."

"And we can help with your dad," said Ian.

This received a confused look from both Alex and Darren.

"What? You think he's just going to let Darren and his sister pack their bags and walk away? We should take him on. We've got the power to help," said Ian.

Alex couldn't argue with Ian's logic, but tackling an adult, a big one at that, could be difficult.

"What could you do? Actually now I think about it, how are you doing any of this?" asked Darren.

Ian's watch started to beep and the Bug Boys took a step back.

Darren watched as the extra arms and wings got sucked back into the boy's bodies. Then he experienced the disgusting aftereffects. A loud fart that sounded like wellies being pulled out of the mud, and a smell similar to milk not fit for drinking. Darren stood up and backed away from the toxic cloud.

"Oh wow, that's rank," said Darren, waving his hand in front of his nose.

"It's complicated," said Alex.

CHAPTER 22

Reddish Brown's Big Day Out

Administrator Reddish Brown made a new friend, but like a lot of great partnerships throughout history, this new relationship didn't start out on the best footing. This was because his new comrade in arms was a robin redbreast, and when the darling little bird first met Reddish, she tried to kill him.

A simple misunderstanding, really. The half-starved bird, desperate for food, decided Reddish Brown's white armour looked close enough to bread as made no difference, and well, the rest is obvious.

Reddish took the attack in his stride. As he ducked and weaved to avoid the Robin's sharp beak, he noticed the poor creature's left leg and tail were tangled with spider web. He deduced this must be throwing off the animal's balance, making flight difficult, likely resulting in a few bad test flights and collisions with trees. This probably disorientated the small creature and made the search for food nearly impossible, so here it was, trying to skewer Reddish.

Once the robin had expelled its last reserves of energy on the visiting Secti, it sat on the ground, its little orange chest rapidly expanding and contracting. Its head was twitching and tilting to take in its surroundings, likely fearful that a predator would take advantage of its weakened condition.

The Secti wondered for a moment if the animal knew the end was nigh and how it was processing the end of its existence. This lead him to ponder his own isolation on Earth, a relatively unknown planet loaded with creatures that could easily end his functions. Without a new robotic body to transfer to, this version of Reddish Brown—the one loaded with knowledge of this planet—would cease to exist. A backup of his consciousness was stored back home so he would eventually re-join the galaxy of the living, but *this* data stream would be no more. This most recent version of "Administrator Reddish Brown" would die.

Watching the robin struggle to breathe and move, Reddish decided to act. There was no reason the creature should end today, as the cause of the bird's dilemma was easily solved. For the first time, Reddish felt a powerful appreciation for life and a deep longing to preserve the bird's existence. An odd, electrical pulse he'd never felt before shot randomly around his body and through his central processing unit. The bird's life actually meant something to him, and he felt bad it was having a tough day. *This is illogical*, thought Reddish.

During Reddish Brown's brief reconnaissance, he had recorded many forms of wildlife and had noted that these particular creatures liked to eat small, wriggly animals that lived underground. So, with a quick wave of one of his arms and an electrostatic pulse from his armour, Reddish was able to trick a few of these squishy creatures to the surface and present them to the robin. The bird quickly snapped them up, and while it was distracted, Reddish removed the tangle of web wrapped around its foot and tail.

With a full belly and working landing gear and rudder, the bird took off.

"You're welcome," grumbled Reddish.

Another odd pulse of current swiftly made its way around his circuitry. He was glad the bird would live a little longer, but also disappointed he'd never see the animal again. *I can't wait to get off this confusing planet*, thought Reddish.

A little later, the tiny robot approached the edge of the woods and saw several massive structures. *These domiciles must be where the humans live*, calculated Reddish. Formed from regular shaped building blocks, the Secti appreciated the effective, if somewhat simplistic design. He wasn't programmed for aesthetic appreciation but found the sharp corners and seemingly hodgepodge rigging of power and data lines quite ugly.

The soft woodland ground suddenly switched to a hard grey surface, likely to aid the large wheeled machines lying dormant at the edges of the stone-like pathway. Reddish walked up to one of the beast's wheels and tapped on the rubber. A pressurized container, likely installed to absorb the changes in the terrain as it rolled to its location. Reddish scanned the rest of the vehicle. A simple internal combustion motor, fuelled by a flammable liquid stored in a large tank at the rear of the vehicle. Reddish pondered why the humans would rely on a mode of transportation that constantly had to be refuelled when the planet's sun could easily provide enough power. *The things we could teach these creatures*, thought Reddish.

As Reddish walked underneath the liquid-powered chariot, he suddenly became aware that he was being watched. A pair of eyes locked on his every move. A huge fur covered creature was hunkered down under the vehicle's motor, its tail, silently moved from left to right and its shoulders slowly bobbed up and down. Reddish suspected its actions were not meant to be friendly. This was a lot bigger than the robin and it was armed with four forward-facing claws on each leg, each one almost as big as the Secti visitor. *This animal could do some damage*, thought Reddish.

134

The Secti quickly cartwheeled back to the rubber wheel and used it for cover. Scanning the area, there weren't many other places to hide. He could climb the vehicle but suspected the creature stalking him could do the same quite easily. He could also make a roll for the woods, but doubted he could outpace the animal. From his quick scans, he surmised this creature had evolved to hunt. It was fast, nimble, and well-armed. There was only one thing for it; he would have to stand and fight and use his superior strength to subdue the animal.

Carefully, Reddish stepped up to the edge of the wheel. He hadn't heard any movement from the furry monster, so chanced a peek.

The Secti came face to face with the hunter. Its intense eyes locked on his, and its mouth opened to reveal several large fangs as it hissed at him. For the first time in his life, Reddish was properly scared. Electrons bounced around his robotic form at twice their normal rate, causing his motors and gears to shudder under the increased power being made available to them. He ducked back behind the tire, but was quickly scooped up by the creature's left paw, and flung back underneath the vehicle.

Disorientated, Reddish had no time to get his bearings before the creature attacked again, using both of its front paws to bat the Secti robot around. Every time he got to his feet, the animal knocked him down again and batted him around some more. Occasionally it stopped to hold Reddish down and feign disinterest, only to once again engage and knock the Secti back and forth between its paws. *Oh, the indignity of it all*, thought Reddish. *I'm being PLAYED WITH!*

Suddenly, his tormenter stopped. Reddish sensed another creature approaching—a human—walking up to and climbing into the vehicle directly above the Secti and his furry puppet master.

Seemingly aware of what happens next, the Secti's tormentor quickly ran away from the vehicle leaving Reddish—a little scratched up but functional—alone between the front and rear wheels of the vehicle.

The metal beast roared to life. First the rapid fire of a small motor near the front of the vehicle, followed by a deep rumble as fuel entered the much larger engine. Reddish, distracted by the noise and vibration, almost didn't see the rear wheel rolling towards him but managed to quickly cartwheel out of the way in time. He watched as the massive chariot made its way down the stone-like pathway, spewing the by-product of its burnt fuel out into the atmosphere.

Uncovered and exposed, Reddish was reminded of his previous dilemma. The large furry monster had been startled by the movement of the vehicle but hadn't forgotten about the little Secti. It was now sitting on a wall looking down at its new toy.

Here we go again, thought Reddish Brown.

As the tower of fanged fury limbered up for another attack, Reddish heard a familiar chirp. He was then suddenly airborne—his top arms firmly held in the claws of the robin redbreast he had saved earlier. His latest attacker could only watch as the Secti and the bird headed back to the woods to the relative safety of the tree tops. *Maybe the winged creature now has the energy to finish me off*, thought Reddish.

The robin descended into the woods and once she got close to the ground, she let go of Reddish and landed. Once back on the woodland floor, she eyed Reddish up and waited. The robin then tapped the ground several times, waited, tapped, waited again. Then she chirped as though getting impatient with the little robot who clearly wasn't getting it.

But Reddish was, and he again scanned the ground for available "wigglies" (his new name for the creatures living in the dirt) before delivering a small electrostatic charge to force them to the surface. Several of them slithered out of the damp soil and the Robin quickly hopped over and devoured them.

"Well, look at you," said Reddish, even though he suspected the creature couldn't understand him. "Could it be we have an arrangement?"

Reddish cartwheeled over to the bird and jumped onto its back. As he suspected, he and the small winged eater of wiggly ground dwellers did seem to have an understanding. Fresh food for a ride, and Reddish couldn't think of a better way to conclude his reconnaissance.

It was time this mission got airborne.

CHAPTER 23

The Rescue Mission

This superhero journey wasn't what Alex thought it would be. In the cartoons it was high on action and destruction, slick costumes and adoring fans. World leaders were supposed to be thanking them for their courage by now, and Rossolington's mayor should be giving them the key to the village, whatever that meant. What would it unlock anyway?

By now there was supposed to be a hot-line for the police to use when they needed the Bug Boys help, or a searchlight in the sky displaying their cool superhero symbol. Maybe the projection of an ant or their "BB" logo. One of the boys would see the symbol and call the other on his walkie-talkie, "This looks like a job for…"

Later, they'd upgrade their lair with all the latest technology and one day, after they got their licenses, they'd even have vehicles like *The Bug Bike* or *The Bugmobile*! This adventure was supposed to be heroes and villains, good against evil. How did it get so complicated?

Just over a week into the superhero business, all they'd managed to do was steal some paperwork and get tangled up in a family drama. Plans to teach Rossolington's top bully a lesson somehow morphed into a rescue mission, and they were even willingly giving Darren the money he asked for.

Alex took a deep breath and put on his orange safety vest. He had managed to get the five pounds they needed to help Darren and his sister get out of Rossolington. Now all they had to do was sneak them out of Darren's house and hopefully avoid a confrontation with Mr. Wilkins.

Darren's plan was surprisingly smart and very simple. Since his father liked to drink after work, he often passed out in front of the television. Darren and his sister would quietly pack some clothes upstairs and simply wait for that to happen. Then, carefully, they'd sneak out the back door and run to the village centre. A bus ride and a train journey later, they'd be back with their mother. Alex and Ian would only be needed if Darren's dad woke up and caused trouble.

Alex really hoped Mr. Wilkins didn't wake up. He felt strong as an ant or a beetle, and nimble when he ate a fly, but none of the bugs he had eaten had prepared him to take on an adult. A big and likely drunk adult at that. Numb, angry, and powerful, and someone that wouldn't hold back if trouble started.

Little Jane Wilkins, all of three years old, sat in her bedroom with her best friend Agatha. Jane was making the best of things. Her room wasn't in desperate need of a coat of paint, it was a pink palace with gold trimmings and paintings of unicorns on the walls. And the broken kids table with a missing leg, propped up with a colouring book, was the centre-piece of a stately dining room. Agatha, with her missing left eye and dirty dress, wasn't the focus of Mr. Wilkins' redirected anger that one time, but the beautiful Duchess Agatha of Rossolington.

"More tea Duchess Agatha?" asked Jane.

"Yes, please," said Jane.

"It's been a lovely day today, hasn't it Agatha?"

"Yes, it has."

Once Jane had filled Agatha's cup with invisible tea, she filled her own and put the pot back on the table. She picked up her cup and took a sip.

"Lovely."

"Yes, lovely."

Jane brushed her greasy blonde hair away from her pretty face. She needed a bath, and her mismatched outfit, consisting of a pink cardigan over her favourite floral pyjamas, needed to be washed. Having run out of tissue, Jane had started to use her sleeves to wipe her snotty nose, starting with the ends, then folding back the wool over the gooeyness to create a fresh piece for later. Her left sleeve was almost at her elbow, but the right one still had some life left in it.

The door to her bedroom opened slowly and Darren silently crept inside, holding his fingers to his mouth for Jane to be quiet. As soon as he was in the room, he carefully closed the door behind him, whispering, "Hey sis, what are you doing?"

"Having tea with Agatha."

"Oh wow, that's nice."

Darren sat down next to his sister on the floor and pulled out a tissue from his back pocket. He wiped the fresh snot leaking out of her nose. "Hey sis, do you want to see mum?"

"Mommy!" squealed Jane.

Darren quickly covered her mouth. "Shhhh, it's a secret. We don't want dad to know. Okay?"

"The mad bear?"

"Yes, the mad bear. He can't know we're going to see mum, so we have to be quiet."

Darren looked around the messy room and spied his mother's old typewriter case underneath Jane's unmade bed. A family heirloom long redundant in the age of computers, it was useful now since all the big suitcases were locked in the attic. The case wasn't huge, but would be big enough to transport a couple of days' worth of clothes. At least enough until a new clean wardrobe could be purchased. Darren reached under the bed and pulled the case out. He opened it up and removed the old blue Royal typewriter.

"Jane, get your shoes please," said Darren.

Jane stood up and started to search the bedroom for her shoes while Darren quickly assembled a full days' worth of clothes for his sister. Jane returned with a white sandal and a red sneaker.

"Jane, they don't match. Can you find a matching shoe?"

"I can't find them."

Frustrated and nervous, Darren quickly latched the now full typewriter case and helped Jane search. Looking under story books and toys left out on the floor, they eventually found the second white sandal, and Darren helped Jane put them on. Looking at his sister, his heart melted. She was in such a state with her snotty sleeves and grubby pyjamas, yet smiled at the thought of seeing mum. Darren wished he could be so hopeful but wondered if they'd even be allowed on the train before someone started to ask questions. Darren had gotten used to adults misreading his age, but travelling with Jane would almost certainly attract attention. He had no choice, though, the situation at home was only getting worse since their mother left. They had to try to leave now or risk the consequences of a rapidly deteriorating relationship with their father, a man made rough and miserable after years of mindless labour in the mine, who then turned to drinking most evenings to forget. The situation at home was a sinking ship, and it was time to find a life boat.

Darren opened Jane's bedroom window. It looked over the backyard and the alleyway beyond the garden's tall wooden fence. Waiting in the alleyway were the Bug Boys. Darren waved, and Alex and Ian waved back. All everyone could do now was wait for Darren's dad to succumb to his routine.

"I still say we should fly them out," said Alex.

"I don't think that would work. For one, we'd make too much noise, and two, I don't fancy the chance I'd drop someone by accident," replied Ian.

The two boys were pacing back and forth in the alley behind Darren's backyard, fully decked out in their orange vests and dust masks, utility belts loaded with flies, ants, earwigs, ladybirds, grasshoppers and even a couple of spiders.

"We need to experiment with flying creatures that don't make so much noise," said Alex.

"Like what?"

"I don't know, wasps maybe. Bees?"

"We'd have to trap them in the vitamin capsules. I don't fancy getting stung. Plus, I don't think they would be any quieter. Once you've got wings like that, they're going to make some noise. A butterfly might work, but I doubt it would make it through undamaged."

Alex tried to picture himself with large colourful butterfly wings and didn't really care for the image. Butterflies and moths were so fragile too; one touch of their wings and they'd be flopping about all over the place. As far as Alex knew, no one ever based a superhero character on a butterfly, and for very valid reasons.

"You're probably right. The stinger would probably poke out from our lower backs too, just like when we tried the earwig," said Alex.

"What are you going to use for this mission?" Ian asked.

"I think I'm going with the ladybird. Tough and strong. You?"

"I like the ants. Strong and quick."

Reddish Brown, astride his trusty robin redbreast, soared high over the village of Rossolington. His reconnaissance mission had gone well and it was time for him to return to the Nest. When he was unable to find his human contacts at their woodland domicile, he fed his winged companion once more, then took to the skies to find his only means of returning home.

He didn't have to travel far before finding them milling about in an alleyway not far from their school. They were waiting for something, and wearing their superhero costumes. The Secti suspected something was about to happen, so guided his bird to a nearby communications pole overlooking the stage set for the boy's latest adventure. *One more log for the records wouldn't hurt*, thought Reddish. How the humans were adapting to the nanobots was fascinating, and their desire to use the technology for good was commendable. The Secti as an advanced race of beings, however, had long understood the corrupting influence of power, and Reddish wondered how long it would take for these young humans to accept the responsibility that came with their new abilities.

It was getting late, and Darren had taken up a positon at the top of the stairs. From this vantage point, he could see most of the living room and the back of his father's head. The television was on but playing the sort of show Darren's dad would never watch, a period drama set when prejudiced and prideful people were still calling the shots. Another indication that Darren's dad had passed out was the untouched beer sitting on the end table next to his drooping hand.

Darren quietly picked up his rucksack and strapped it to his back. He then went back into Jane's room to find her patiently sitting on her typewriter case.

"It's time to go, sis," whispered Darren.

Jane stood up and picked up Agatha. Darren grabbed her case.

"Ok, remember, be very quiet."

Jane nodded, and Darren led the way out of the room. Slowly but surely, they crept downstairs one step at a time, taking care to avoid the areas of each step they knew would creak. So far, so good.

They slowly and carefully made their way behind the sofa where their dad sat, unconscious. Jane walked ahead into the kitchen while Darren took one final look at his father. The ash tray on the end table was full of cigarette butts and there were several empty beer bottles next to it. Darren noticed his father's other hand holding a burning cigarette, and it was almost to the nub.

The heat from the dying cigarette burned Mr. Wilkins' fingers and he bolted out of the chair, frantically shaking his hand. Getting his bearings, he saw Darren run into the kitchen and scoop up Jane.

"Where the bloody hell are you going?"

The back door to the house flew open, and Darren, carrying his sister, ran out into the backyard, closely followed by their dad.

Darren shouted, "ALEX! IAN!"

Still carrying Jane, Darren made it to the end of the yard and unlocked the gate. But he wasn't able to get any further as his dad grabbed his collar. Darren let go of Jane and she fell to the floor. She backed away from the two men, her little feet pushing against the uncut lawn until she was pressed against the fence. She screamed when her dad slapped Darren across the face, sending him halfway across the yard back towards the house. She screamed again when she saw Ian, with his large ant-like eyes and shiny antennae.

"It's okay, Jane, the Bug Boys are here to help," said Ian, trying to calm her down.

Mr. Wilkins took off his belt as he walked over to Darren lying on the lawn.

"That's it, boy, it's time you had a good hiding."

"I don't think so!" said Alex, the now human-ladybird hybrid. He leapt up onto Mr. Wilkins' back and wrapped all four arms around him.

"Darren, RUN!"

Darren scrambled on all fours over to Jane and held her. Ian ran over to Alex to help.

With the weight of Alex on his back, and still intoxicated from the beer, Mr. Wilkins lost his balance and fell backwards. His overweight body slammed Alex hard into the ground, causing him to lose his grip as he was temporarily winded. Mr. Wilkins rolled over, and as he got up, blindly swung his belt at Alex, catching him with the buckle across the lip. The action created a deep cut and blood started to gush down Alex's face.

Ian rushed Mr. Wilkins and tackled him to the ground. Before the lout had time to respond, Ian brought all four fists down hard onto Mr. Wilkins' chest, causing the big man to growl in pain. The attack, however, didn't do much. Ian was strong now, but Mr. Wilkins was a big *well-padded* man.

Hurt but not done, Mr. Wilkins swung his left arm and clouted Ian across the face with the back of his fist. Ian screamed out in pain and rolled over away from Mr. Wilkins holding his jaw. It was broken. The pain Ian felt was incredible but was quickly replaced with the pins and needles sensation the boys had gotten used to over the last few days. Those little nanobots in his system were now rushing around the damaged area making repairs.

Mr. Wilkins got to his feet. It was the first time he got to properly take in the scene playing out in his backyard. Two kids, in safety gear from the pit, with extra arms and weird eyes. Were they bugs? Mr. Wilkins was no light-weight when it came to drinking, but he'd never hallucinated before. In the back corner of the yard, his son and daughter held on to each other.

Alex got to his feet, and Mr. Wilkins stared in disbelief as he watched the blood on Alex's face crawl back into his busted lip.

Alex was angry. There they were again, losing to the bully. Ian was on the floor, holding his jaw and Alex's first move had done nothing. They had all the strength they needed but didn't know how to use it.

Remembering how tough his back got when he was transformed into a ladybird, Alex ran at Mr. Wilkins and smashed his shoulder into the big man's gut. The effect was like hitting the lout with a brick wall, and Mr. Wilkins flew back and slammed into the house. His head snapped back and caught the corner of the kitchen window, which smashed and sent shards of glass down over the dazed man. Some of the pieces caught his exposed arms and cut the skin in several places.

Ian joined Alex, rubbing his now fully repaired jaw.

Mr. Wilkins, shaken now but not totally out of the game, looked a mess. Dirty, beaten, dizzy and bloody. He dropped his belt and examined his arms. Some of the cuts were very deep and would require stitches. Breathing hard, he held out his hand to say he'd had enough. The big man's eye drooped, and then closed. Mr. Wilkins fell to the ground, unconscious.

Darren was unaccustomed to seeing his dad beaten like this. The towering figure in his life, worked over by a couple of kids from his school. Darren couldn't help it, he felt sorry for his dad, and then hated himself for it. "Okay, he's had enough."

"What do we do now?" asked Ian.

Darren carried Jane into the house and told her to go back to her room. When he reappeared in the yard, he was carrying a phone and a twenty-pound note.

"You two had better go, I have to call for an ambulance."

Darren handed the money to Ian. "Here, I don't think I'll be needing this now. Don't worry, I'll say he got drunk and fell into the window."

"Are you sure?" asked Alex.

"Yeah. It's not like it's hard to believe."

The boys carefully but quickly made their way back to the woods and their base of operations. Neither said a word to each other as they replayed the evening's events back in their minds over and over again. Nothing had gone according to plan. Darren wasn't on a train going to see his mum, and they still had Donald Brock's filing cabinet. As they reached the twenty-minute mark, the stomach pain and resulting gas leak was just the rancid icing on the turd cake of their day.

"What if Darren's dad dies?" asked Ian.

Alex looked shocked. "He won't. Will he?"

"I don't know. I've never seen that much blood before."

Alex and Ian thought about that for a moment. What if Mr. Wilkins died? He was a bad man for sure, but did he deserve to die? The boys for a moment selfishly thought about what that meant for them. What if they had killed someone? What if there were witnesses? A nosy neighbour watching everything from their bedroom window. Should Alex and Ian tell someone, and what would they say? Would they be taken to jail or a laboratory?

"I don't know about you Ian but I think I'm done with this superhero lark."

CHAPTER 24

The Aftermath Pizza

The next day at Robin Bank wasn't like any other day. There were classes and playground antics, of course, the usual school business, but Alex and Ian kept to themselves. They didn't raise their hands to offer up the right answers, or make any effort to contribute to class discussions—much to the chagrin of their teachers who had quickly gotten used to the novelty of having, not one, but two motivated students.

The world didn't feel solid anymore, and all Alex and Ian could think about was Mr. Wilkins and Darren. The image of Mr. Wilkins' big, bloody body holding out his hand before falling to the ground tormented them. At any moment they expected police cars to come speeding into the school parking lot, sirens blazing and lights flashing. Rossolington's two constables, Smith and Walker, would be leading a team of armed police from the neighbouring villages, to arrest the dangerous villains known as the Bug Boys. It wasn't, however, until after school and they were close to home that the events of the previous evening came back to haunt them.

Alex noticed first and grabbed Ian's arm. "Look."

Parked in front of Alex's house was Smith and Walker's tiny police car, and right behind that, the car Alex would never be allowed to drive again. His dad was home early from his business trip, and Alex had a pretty good idea why. This was it, they were done. They'd be arrested, thrown in jail with the key lost forever. Alex pictured a hospital room and the sound of a heart rate monitor logging the last beats of Mr. Wilkins' life on earth. The mental scene then cut to Darren helping the police draw sketches of Ian-ant and Alex-ladybird.

"What do we do?" asked Ian.

"I don't know."

"Maybe we should go in. We'd at least know what happened to Mr. Wilkins."

"Yeah, but what if Darren told on us? We'll go to jail!"

The boys were just a few meters away from Ian's house and were startled when Ian's dad emerged holding a piece of paper. The boys quickly hid behind the nearest parked car.

Mr. Harris closed the front door and locked it. Using some tape, he attached the folded piece of paper to the door. After that, he walked into the street and then over to Alex's house.

"Oh my God, my dad's in on it too! We're done for," said Ian.

Once Mr. Harris had been let into the Adam's household, the two boys scurried over to Ian's front door and grabbed the note. It was for Ian, it said so on the cover.

> *Ian. Over at ~~Al's~~, ~~Albert~~, ~~Alonso's~~, your friend's house.*
> *Go there when you get home from school. Dad.*

"This is bad," said Ian.

"What do we do now?" asked Alex. "They're expecting us any minute."

"We could run! That's right, run for it. We've got superpowers now. We don't have to stay here and face the music, we did nothing wrong. Let's eat a fly and take off! We could be in Scotland in no time. Bollocks to this hero rubbish, we could become outlaws. Highland outlaws!"

"What is wrong with you?" Alex exclaimed. "Don't be daft, and calm down. I say we go in. Darren said he would take care of everything, so let's trust him."

"And what if Darren sold us out?"

Alex had to admit that was a possibility. What did they really know about Darren? Just two days ago they were ready to teach that bully a lesson; a few days before that Darren was beating them up in the woods, and now they were counting on his honesty.

The choice between staying to face the music and flying off to Scotland to be kilt-wearing highway bugs, wasn't really a choice at all. Alex started walking towards his house, and Ian reluctantly followed.

"Really, we're going in?" said Ian. "Think about it, please. We could use the twenty pounds to buy supplies, and then get our gear from the base. I've stocked up on flies, too. We flew around Rosso in a few seconds in our tests, we'd easily get to Scotland in under an hour."

"Stop it, we're not going to Scotland."

Once the boys reached the front door, they stopped. Alex turned to Ian. "Just try to stay calm and quiet. Okay?"

Alex opened the door and the boys walked into the house.

In the living room, Alex and Ian were confronted by a sea of adults. Alex's mum and dad; Ian's dad, Mr. Harris; and the constables, Smith and Walker. There was also another lady the boys had never seen before, sitting on the sofa sipping a cup of tea. As Alex led the boys into the living room, Sharon got up, still wearing her paisley dressing gown, and rushed over to Alex to give him a big hug. Alex initially took this as a good sign until his mind hijacked that thought, and he then assumed his mother was getting in one last hug before he was carted off to jail.

"Oh thank goodness you're okay," said Sharon.

"You boys okay?" asked Constable Smith as he stood with Walker, his thumbs wedged between his belt and sizable belly. Alex took a moment to ponder how two men that large managed to fit inside their tiny police car. Maybe one sat in the back.

"Err, yeah, we're fine," said Alex.

"Why didn't you tell us about Mr. Wilkins?" asked Sharon.

Alex shared a glance with Ian and wished he could secretly confer with his friend like the Secti do. "Err, well, err, we thought it was private," said Alex.

Constables Walker and Smith nodded in approval, and Alex's dad smiled a "that's my boy" smile. *Phew, that must have been the right thing to say*, thought Alex.

"Hello," said the new lady on the sofa. "My name is Mrs. Prickle, I'm with social services." She put her cup of tea down and stood up. If Alex were to describe what a social services person looked like, he would have described her. She was a huge folder full of paperwork that had grown legs and arms. "I was contacted after your friend Darren called for an ambulance last night. He said you were both witnesses to Mr. Wilkins' behaviour?"

Alex told the truth. "Yes, we saw what Mr. Wilkins did."

Technically that wasn't a lie. If Mrs. Prickle asked if Alex and Ian had tried to bust Darren out of his suburban prison, he'd have to make something up, but for now, it was easier to play along and respond to her questions with basic answers. No fluff or extra information. He remembered getting that advice from a TV show about lawyers once. Sharon increased the pressure of her hug and cradled Alex's head.

"Yes, well, it seems, as you likely saw, that Mr. Wilkins wasn't keeping a happy, healthy home. So after last night's events, we wanted to make sure you were both okay. It can't have been easy to see a grown man act like that," said Mrs. Prickle.

Ian walked over to his dad, and Tom put his arm around Ian's shoulders. "It was weird, but Darren took care of it."

"How are Darren and his sis?" asked Alex.

"Oh, they're fine. Once we took Mr. Wilkins into custody, we had someone call Mrs. Wilkins. She's on her way back and should be home soon. We've got some people around the house now cleaning up. What a mess," said Mrs. Prickle.

There wasn't a device made that could measure the relief Alex was feeling. Mr. Wilkins was alive and where he belonged, and Darren and his sister were being reunited with their mother. Alex felt great for Darren and looked forward to seeing him at school. *My goodness I'm actually looking forward to seeing Darren,* thought Alex.

"Right, well," said constable Smith. "It seems everything's all square here, we'll get out of your hair. Thank you for your time, everyone."

The two officers and Mrs. Prickle left the house via the front door and headed for their police car. Alex, curious about the seating order in the tiny vehicle—rushed over to the living room window to watch them drive away. It was exactly how he pictured it. Smith got in the front, and Walker in the back on the opposite side of the car to balance out the weight. Poor Mrs. Prickle took the front passenger seat. The car's engine wheezed and putted as it struggled to haul the trio down York Street.

"Okay Ian, time for tea," said Tom. "Thank you Mr. and Mrs. Adams, for your hospitality."

"Perfect," exclaimed Sharon. "Let's order pizza!"

Alex looked at Ian, and then Ian looked at his dad. Tom tried not to look at anyone, but it didn't matter because Frank took care of it. "Tom, you and Ian are welcome to join us."

Tom looked at Ian's pleading face. "Err, sure, that'll be great."

CHAPTER 25

Shockwave

It was Thursday, 6:30 a.m. Alex counted the morning wake-up routine on his fingers. Pee, one. FART, two. Giggle, three.

Sharon shouted, "Frank Adams!" That was four.

"Oh wow, I needed that," sighed Frank. *All five present and correct*, thought Alex.

The sound of this morning's methane explosion was akin to Ringo Star wailing on a drum set made of frogs—a horrible, wet sounding patter accompanied by a throaty "bwarp!" Alex snuggled under his sheets and smiled; it was nice to have dad back again.

Frank was happy to say goodbye to that night's gas collection. While he was away, he had made the most of the free lunches, dinners, and snacks and easily gained half a stone as he slept through redundant lectures on safety in the workplace. Left unmonitored by Sharon, he spent time with other conference attendees at various pubs close to the convention hall to bemoan how pointless the day's lectures were and complain how badly their companies were run, simultaneously billing anything and everything back to their respective employers. It was like having your cake and eating it, then complaining that it wasn't as good as what mum used to make. Good times.

Back at home, Frank was happy to get back into his routine and was looking forward to his first day back at the pit. The place had been eerily quiet while he was away. He hadn't received a single call or email about any safety-related matter at the mine, which was unusual. There was always someone with a suggestion, or a minor miner accident that had to be logged. Most of his communications with the pit crews were negative, at best biting ridicule. So to say Frank was suspicious about what he'd find when he got to work was an understatement.

After the customary fight for the bathroom, followed by Sharon's morning inspection and breakfast, Frank drove Graham and Robert to St. Peter's primary school, before making his way to the pit.

As he pulled into his parking space, his suspicions about the mine were further confirmed. His parking sign had remained undamaged the entire time he was away. If his parking sign hadn't seen any attention, that meant something else did.

Word of his arrival in the village might not have travelled the unofficial Rosso gossip network yet. So if there were shenanigans, he was set perfectly to surprise whomever and whatever. Frank decided to skip visiting his not-really-an-office and made straight for the cage room. As a keen Geotech Engineer and safety officer, Frank could sense when people were doing something they shouldn't. It was something in their sweat perhaps, a pheromone that chanted "please don't get caught, please don't get caught."

For as long as Frank had known Gladice, he'd never seen her look nervous, but today she was clearly shaken by his arrival.

Just before the shaft elevator doors closed, he saw Gladice dive for her phone. He'd honestly never seen the octogenarian move that fast before, and Frank smiled the smile made when knowing he was going to catch someone doing something they shouldn't. Adding up Donald Brock's drive for more profits with the miners' willingness to break the rules for a bonus, Frank already had a good idea what was happening.

Arriving at the new seam a couple of minutes later, Frank stepped out of the elevator and sighed. He was right, the seam had been worked quickly with little regard for safety. Room after room at the wrong ratio, with only a handful of extra supports brought in to support the space. The walls crackled and snapped under the weight of 1,600 meters of earth, rock, and coal above it. The tough metal supports groaned under the pressure. This was a time bomb.

Frank stepped further into the seam and started to explore. He placed his hand over one of the motor housings that ran the conveyor belt responsible for transporting coal out of the mine. Still hot. Gladice may have been able to call down and warn them of his arrival, but there was no way they could have shut down the equipment and get to one of the other elevators to make their escape. Frank walked further into the seam, scanning left and right for signs of life. A few rooms in, he started to hear activity. As he passed each pillar, he could faintly hear shuffling and whispers from the adjacent rooms. Someone was trying to sneak past him to get back to the elevators. As Frank carefully tracked back to catch them in the act, he heard voices coming from the deepest part of the seam. Loud voices, but just for a moment—a quickly silenced argument. One of the voices sounded like Mike, so Frank decided to go after the leader instead of the worker bees trying to skulk away.

The mine made Frank nervous. He was used to the regular sounds a mine made, but this was different. It was like a giant slowly waking up in a bad mood. The coal pillars were struggling and loudly complaining about the extra work they were being forced to do. Frank felt the ground beneath him shake for a moment, and coal dust fell from the ceiling. He wanted to leave, but he needed to reach the voices he'd just heard. Frank's number one priority now was to get everyone top-side. The punishments for violating safety protocols could wait.

At the end of the seam, Frank found Mike and a handful of miners setting up another piece of support equipment. Being so far into the mine, they clearly didn't get the warning about Frank's arrival, and once they were aware, they assumed the posture of six-year-olds who had been caught with their hands in the biscuit tin. They shuffled nervously and looked at the ground.

"Everybody out. Now," said Frank.

The small group of men silently walked past Frank, none of them could look him in the eye. Mike brought up the rear, and Frank grabbed his arm. "Let's talk."

Once alone, Frank let Mike have it. "What the hell are you doing, Mike?"

The walls seemed to reflect Frank's mood, groaning and popping even louder than before. The ground shook again and coal debris felt from the ceiling and rattled against the metal support. Mike looked at the ground as he responded. "We just wanted to meet the new quota, Frank."

"Oh, is that right?" said Frank. "Do you hear that? The walls? This place is a death trap and you of all people should know better!"

"I'm sorry. Mr. Brock had these piles of cash on his desk. Started talking about the wife's holidays. Then Samantha got excited about the South of France. I got confused."

Right above the two men came a loud snapping sound, like a bullwhip being cracked, and Frank looked up to see a large crack appear in the ceiling. The ground shook again and another crack appeared, branching off from the first one, heading back towards the exit to the seam. A large chunk of coal crashed onto the floor beside the two men and the hole in the ceiling above them got longer and wider. Frank grabbed Mike's safety vest and pulled him towards the metal support. The ground didn't stop shaking this time, and Frank watched the corridor leading from the room they were in. New cracks formed in the ceiling all the way down the corridor, and then, after a thunderous blast, the ceiling became the floor.

The resulting shockwave from the collapse blasted Frank and Mike further into their room and knocked them off their feet. They were sealed in, and beyond their new tomb, they could hear explosion after explosion. Millions of tons of solid fuel, super-heated by friction, bursting into flames. Rossolington's colliery was dying, and wasn't going down quietly.

The shockwave made its way down Alexandra Road, bouncing off red brick houses and shaking spotless windows in the connecting streets. The wave rudely invaded people's gardens and knocked over milk bottles. The blast was short-lived, but brutal, and everyone who felt it knew exactly what had caused it. It rattled the bike sheds at Robin Bank Academy, set off car alarms, and blew the ice cream off Mrs. Pratchett's 99 Flake, as she and the Bonny Village judges were taking a break by Mr. Whippy's van by the entrance to York Street.

The shockwave made Sharon spill her cup of tea. She picked up her little black book, found the page she was working on, and crossed out 836. She put a zero next to it. The heading at the top of the page read, "Good Pit Days."

The plastic soldiers doing battle at Britannica Pass fell over. Alex picked up his favourite, whom he had named Private Hopkins, and turned to Ian. "The mine."

The force of the blast was enough to force Donald Brock's paintings off the wall, and his poorly reinstalled upside-down window fell out of its frame and landed on the colliery roof. Donald fell into his expensive chair and selfishly thought about taking his private elevator to his private parking space to make a run for it. He wasn't stupid; he knew he'd pushed his luck with the new seam, and now that it had run out, it was maybe time to disappear. It wouldn't be long before Frank reported him to the authorities and his executive man-cave was swapped out for a Graybar hotel.

Donald got up and shuffled over to his window overlooking the office. The space was emptying fast as everyone rushed outside. Natalie burst into the office, her hair still defying gravity but unsure of which direction to go. "Mr. Brock! The mine!"

"Oh really, are you sure?" asked Donald sarcastically. "Where's Frank Adams?"

"I haven't seen him, Mr. Brock. I thought he was away on business."

That's right, thought Donald, Mike had sent him away to some pointless all-expenses-paid safety convention. There may still be a way out of this mess.

"Where's Mike Ridley?" asked Donald.

"I don't know, he was in this morning," Natalie cupped her hands over her mouth in horror. "Oh my sainted-aunt, he's probably still in the mine."

Donald put his arm around Natalie's shoulders and escorted her out of his office. "Okay let's not panic. How about you ask around and find out for sure. There's a good girl."

Natalie left and Donald sat down to do some serious conniving. With Frank out of town, and Mike possibly dead, there was a way out of this mess. Donald could hear the sound of sirens getting closer. The entire village was likely heading this way. He straightened his tie and grabbed his jacket. It was time to do some damage control. He just needed to find the miners who had worked the new seam and appeal to their wallets.

After the jolt from the mine explosion ended the latest campaign at Britannica Pass, Alex and Ian ran to their lair to get suited up. They didn't talk; Alex was lost in his own thoughts and Ian didn't disturb him. Alex always knew the mine was a dangerous place, but figured if anyone could keep it safe, it was his dad. Alex had no idea what, if anything, they could do to help, but putting on the orange vests and bug-filled utility belts made him feel a little better.

Administrator Reddish Brown joined them as they left their lair, tucking himself into one of Ian's pockets to stay out of sight. Ian used some tape to attach the Secti's universal translator radio to his utility belt.

People poured out of York Street, Charles Street, Edge Way and Harbor Lane into Alexandra Road. Most on foot, some in cars. The boys caught up with Alex's mum as she made her way to the pit.

"Hi mum," said Alex.

Sharon, still in her paisley dressing gown and fluffy pink slippers, gave Alex a big hug.

"What on earth are you wearing?" asked Sharon.

She took a step back to take it all in.

"We were playing a superhero game before school, Mrs. Adams," said Ian.

Sharon shook her head and rolled her eyes. Alex could tell she didn't really care; they all had more important things to worry about.

"Well I'm glad you're here, Alex. Graham and Robert are being kept at school for the time being. I'm sick with worry. If your dad's stuck in that bloody mine, I'll bloody kill him!"

The scene at the colliery's parking lot was chaotic. There was an odd mix of feelings hanging in the air. The miners who had escaped to avoid Frank's wrath knew full well why the mine had collapsed. The screams of joy from their families, happy to see them alive, were bittersweet and stung. Those feelings got worse once Sharon appeared with Alex. The village folk gave her room and avoided eye contact. Sharon looked at everyone and didn't want to believe she knew why. Natalie walked up to her to spell it out.

"Frank's down there."

Donald Brock grabbed his cell phone, took his elevator to his private parking space and exited the building through a side door. He crept up behind the scene developing in the parking lot. From his vantage point, he could see the miners that had escaped and the police keeping the crowds away from the cage room as the local fire brigade unpacked their hoses. He had to work quickly before one of the miners talked to the newspaper reporters, who were likely only minutes away.

As he figured out the best way to get to them without causing too much fuss, he saw two boys dressed in orange safety vests. Very similar safety gear worn by the two thieves bouncing around his security video with his filing cabinet.

Alex tapped Ian on the arm. "I've got an idea."

"What's that?"

"I think we can help, but we can't do it from here."

"We can't leave your mum. She'll go spare if you leave now."

"That can't be helped."

While Alex's mum and Natalie talked, Alex took a step back, and then another. Ian followed. This continued, one experimental step at a time. Once they were a few meters away and still not missed, they turned and ran.

"Where are we going?" asked Ian.

"To the woods, we have to get behind the mine where we won't be seen."

"Seen doing what?" asked Ian.

"Mining!"

CHAPTER 26

Tally-Bally-Ho!

Donald Brock saw the two boys sprinting out of the parking lot. There was no way he was going to catch them on foot, so he headed back to his private garage and jumped into his car. The expensive automobile rumbled to life, gobbling up fuel to power its eight-cylinder engine. He pressed a button on his rear view mirror and the garage door directly ahead slowly opened.

Donald pulled out of the colliery and took a left turn on Homes Karr Road. As he turned right onto Alexandra Road, he drove past a small convoy of news vans headed in the opposite direction. Leaving the pit probably wasn't the best course of action, but his sizable gut was telling him those two kids had his paperwork. If he could recover that, there would be no evidence that he ordered the extra work at the mine, or anything to explain where the extra coal was going. It would be his word against a few miners, who were not likely to implicate themselves anyway. The explosion would just be "one of those unfortunate things" that happens at a coal mine from time to time. And all the people who knew better would be eager to jump on that story thread. As far as Donald knew, the only person that could potentially spoil that scenario wasn't even in town.

The two kids were moving fast and turned left onto York Street. Donald saw them ahead but wasn't able to follow them as his access was blocked by a Mr. Whippy ice-cream van and that insufferable Mrs. Pratchett complaining about her ruined ice cream. He would have to drive ahead, take a left on Oxford Street and hope the kids hadn't gone into one of the houses.

As Donald drove down Oxford Street, he saw the boys leave York Street and head straight for the woods. *Perfect,* thought Donald. It was time to make his move.

Donald planted his fat foot on the gas and the mighty car jolted forward overtaking the kids just as they reached the entrance to the woods. He turned and cut them off, then as quickly as he could, climbed out of the car. The two boys split up and tried to run around both ends of the vehicle, but Donald managed to grab one by the safety vest he was wearing. He grabbed the kid's ear and held it hard while calling out for the other boy. "Oy! Stop right there!"

What is it with bullies and the ear grabbing? thought Alex as Mr. Brock called out to Ian. Ian complied and walked back over to Mr. Brock's car.

"Where are you boys going?" asked Mr. Brock.

"None of your business!" said Alex.

"Oh, is that right? Well I've got security footage of you two stealing a filing cabinet from the colliery."

Alex and Ian stared at each other, as good as confirming their guilt. Did Mr. Brock really have them on tape? They knew their miscalculations that evening might have been recorded, but figured since they weren't exactly themselves, they thought they might have gotten away with it.

"That's theft and damage to private property. You reinstalled my window upside down!"

Alex frowned at Ian, who just shrugged.

"So where is it? Is it in the woods?"

Alex couldn't free his ears from Mr. Brock's firm grip. "Yes, now let go of me!"

"Oh, I don't think so. Not until I see my paperwork."

Alex locked eyes with Ian and quickly glanced towards the woods. Ian nodded and started to run.

"Oy!" shouted Mr. Brock, but Ian was already gone.

Disappointed but not done, Mr. Brock dragged Alex by his ear into the woods. "You better not be messing with me kid."

A few minutes later, Mr. Brock pushed Alex into the lair and walked over to his filing cabinet.

"I knew it! What's all this sticky stuff you've got covering it?"

Alex just shrugged.

As Mr. Brock started to claw at the web covering the filing cabinet, Alex looked up to see a silhouette forming on the blue tarp ceiling. Alex took a couple of steps back to the lair's entrance way.

"Mr. Brock, do you like spiders?"

"What?"

Alex pointed at the tarp above Mr. Brock. As large as life and twice as scary, there appeared the outline of a massive spider. Easily a meter wide, its six upper legs started scratching and thumping the tarp, causing the entire lair to shake. Mr. Brock rubbed the sticky substance he'd pulled off the filing cabinet with his fingers, then looked up in terror. His worst, most primal fears realized, he screamed in such a way that would make little girls think he was a wuss.

166

"Red, can you scan the ground for insects?" asked Ian.

"Of course," said Administrator Reddish Brown.

"Great, then scan for this." Ian opened an encyclopaedia to a page he'd marked earlier. Since the boys were still curious about the abilities they could get from other bugs, and the Secti were eager to build a new eco system for them in the Nest, Ian took it upon himself to research bugs available in their neck of the woods. The page he was showing Reddish described Mining Bees, which would likely be dormant in spring, located underground in individual burrows.

"No problem," said Reddish in his high-pitched munchkin voice coming from the small transistor radio still attached to Ian's utility belt. "I have logged those very creatures during my travels. They're on my menu of insects the Secti would like you to transport to the Nest."

"We don't have time for this, Ian!" Alex said. "My dad's trapped in the mine, and his safety kit is only good for about an hour. We've got to go. Ant power will do."

"Alex, these are MINING BEES. This is what they do. They dig. Reddish, please find us some," said Ian.

"Listen to your friend," said Reddish. "These creatures would seem to be more effective diggers, and should help you accomplish your task a lot faster. I can point you in the right direction, assuming of course your target is still functioning."

Alex glared at Reddish. "Still functioning? That's my dad you're talking about, you stupid little robot!"

"Jeez Red, I thought you Secti were super smart," said Ian.

As far as Reddish Brown could show it, he realized his error. "My apologies. I didn't mean to sound insensitive."

"Fine," said Alex, still a little irritated. "Can we please get going?"

Reddish Brown jumped off the dressing table and cartwheeled out into the woods. Alex and Ian followed. Once

Reddish was a few meters in front of the two boys, the robin redbreast, who had stayed away while she sensed the boys nearby, swooped down and joined Reddish on the ground. Alex and Ian held back so as not to startle it, and watched in amazement as Reddish Brown conjured up earthworms from the soil for the (surprisingly plump for its size) bird. After the robin had quickly polished off its meal, Reddish jumped on its back and the two took off. Alex and Ian (who was still sporting spider power) ran after the now airborne alien insectoid robot.

A short time later, Reddish led them to the location where he had found the most mining bees. After emptying one of their utility belt containers, and thereby setting a bunch of happy earwigs free, the boys carefully collected three mining bees each and stored them away. They were happy to note the bugs were a little groggy and uninterested in stinging them, even after having their spring nap interrupted. With that done, it was time for the Bug Boys to save Alex's dad.

In the woods directly behind the mine, Alex turned to Reddish. "Right, can you scan for my dad and tell me where he is?"

Reddish Brown jumped down from his robin, and held out his arms. "There are two large lifeforms below us, by earth measurements, 1,598.67 meters below, and 102.345 meters directly ahead. You will need to dig-"

"A 1,601-meter tunnel at approximately three point five degrees," said Ian. After seeing Alex's reaction, he said, "What? I like trigonometry now."

"You will need to start digging right where I'm standing. As you make progress, I will make new calculations and correct your trajectory."

"Okay, good," said Alex. He reached for the container holding the mining bees and carefully placed one in the palm of his hand. The confused insect slowly walked across Alex's palm. Opening his mouth wide, Alex threw the creature to the back of his throat and swallowed.

The transformation was immediate. First, a beautiful, long set of wings poked through the hole cut out of the back of Alex's safety vest. Then a set of antennae popped out of his forehead, his eyes got larger and turned black and shiny. The extra arms appeared next, and Alex had to agree with Ian on this insect choice. With other bugs the boys had swallowed, the extra arms were just copies of the originals, but with the mining bee, all his arms and legs got a wicked upgrade. Alex flexed all his chunky arms and felt incredibly strong.

The transformation, however, was not over and Alex felt the pins and needles sensation reach his tail bone. As they suspected, the nanobots, doing the best they could to combine both Alex and the bee, decided in their programmed wisdom to include the stinger, and use his tail bone as its anchor. The sharp brown stinger poked out just above Alex's shorts, and he gave it a wiggle.

Alex walked over to where Reddish Brown was standing. He knelt down and punched the ground with all four fists. With his added strength, he easily cut into the soil and was able to lift a meter-wide chunk off the ground away from the dig site. "Right, Ian. As soon as you stop being a spider, get changed and follow me in. I'll dig, and you can take the dirt to the surface. Red, you keep a watch on our direction."

"I will," said Reddish. "If you can keep up this pace, you'll reach the buried humans in, by earth measurements, fifty minutes and thirty-two seconds."

Alex looked at Ian. They had wasted too much time with Mr. Brock and obtaining the bees. They would need to work fast to get there in time.

"Tally-Bally-Ho," said Alex.

CHAPTER 27

Trapped

Frank and Mike coughed as the coal dust settled in their newly formed tomb. Above them, they could hear rumblings as the upper layers of the mine collapsed and settled. It was hot in their cave and the lights on their hard hats had been smashed when the blast of air and debris hit them. Frank fumbled in the dark for his kit and found his torch. Turning it on, he could see the only reason both men were still alive was due to the metal support Mike and his crew installed. A large slab of rock had fallen from the old ceiling and was held up at an angle by the support. The resulting wedge-shaped space was barely a meter tall, and approximately four meters long. Mike groaned.

"You okay Mike?"

Frank pointed his torch at Mike, and saw that his ankle was trapped under the rocks that had sealed them in the room. Mike tried to shift his weight onto his elbows to crawl free, but he couldn't do it. The small cave rumbled again.

"Don't move, you might bring down the roof."

"Really?" asked Mike. "Is that what we're worried about?"

Frank sensed his friend's frustration. The air was getting thick with coal dust, carbon dioxide, and methane. The latter was the most dangerous—one spark could turn their room into a furnace. Frank located Mike's safety kit and unpacked his air tank and face mask. After connecting the tubes between the mask and tank, he placed the mask over Mike's mouth and opened the valve to the pressurized container.

"Breathe easy, try not to get worked up."

Frank assembled his own face mask and tank and turned on the air. The valve hissed a little, and he took a couple of deep breaths.

"Don't get worked up," said Mike. "We're screwed, Frank, and you know it."

"I don't know any such thing."

"Ha, you're kidding yourself. I've managed to bury us a mile underground. There's no way we're getting out."

Frank looked up at their new ceiling. Above them was a mile of rock, coal, toxic gases and fire. It was unlikely anyone could reach them before their oxygen ran out. "Are you sure? The shaft might still be intact. If the rescue crew can use that to get most of the way here, they might be able to find a way to us."

"Okay, sure, whatever you say Frank. We'll make it, easy peasy." Mike shifted to his side and winced as the rocks pressed down on his ankle. "Well, at least I don't have to worry about going on that bloody holiday now."

"Where are you going?"

"Well, if we'd met our quota, the wife wanted to go to nice."

"Nice?"

"Yeah, it's French. In the south."

Frank smiled. "You wolly, that's Nice, pronounced *niece*. I've been there. Lovely part of the world."

"When did you get to go there?"

"Before Sharon and I had the boys. When Robert gets a little older we're planning to go again. I miss travelling. The boys need to see a bit of the world."

Mike shook his head. "Too much trouble if you ask me, I'd rather stay at home. There's nothing over there that we don't have here. I don't see the point."

"Then why were you going?"

"Samantha wants to go. That's all she ever talks about; it's an obsession. Bloody holiday brochures on the dining room table, year in year out. I swear she's only happy when she's spending my money. Well, she'll have to find someone else to pay for her stuff now."

"I'm sure she's not that bad," said Frank, who actually knew better. He'd met Samantha once at a company function and it was clear her interest in Mike was purely financial.

"Yes she is," said Mike. "I bet, right now, the entire village is upstairs worrying about us. I bet your Sharon and the boys are worried sick. Samantha is probably digging out my life insurance policy."

Mike shifted his weight again and rested on his back, placing his hands on his belly. Frank thought about his boys.

"I let Alex drive home the other day."

"Really? How'd that go?"

"He did great; a little distracted for some reason, but he pulled into York Street and took that right turn towards our house almost perfectly."

"Did he enjoy it?"

"I think so. I don't think Graham and Robert were too thrilled, but it was nice. He'll be driving full-time in a few years."

Mike tilted his head back and saw Frank staring at the floor. A look of loss in his eyes.

"You'll get to see that, Frank. Right now the rescue crew are heading down the shaft, and before you know it, we'll hear them tapping on this wall."

Frank appreciated the gesture and nodded. "We had better cut down on the chit chat and conserve our air."

"Sure Frank. Whatever you say."

In the woods behind the Rossolington colliery, the Bug Boys were hard at work digging their tunnel. Thirty minutes had passed and they were making great progress. Alex led the dig, punching and scraping as hard and fast as he could, while Ian transported the coal and rocks up to the surface. As they dug, Reddish Brown guided the boys towards their target. The only difficulty so far occurred during Alex's change back to being a regular boy. That much gas released in such a tight space proved to be an eye-watering event, and Ian had to use his mining bee wings to mix up the rancid air with the good stuff.

This method for ventilation proved even more useful as the boys got deeper. The mine was awash with all manner of toxic chemicals, so as Alex dug, he flapped his wings to push the gases upward and out of their tunnel. When Ian reached the surface, he made sure he pushed fresh air back down.

They were getting close. They had reached many of the previously mined seams, and Alex started to find tools and equipment amongst the soil, rock and coal. Thankfully, he had not discovered any miners. Reddish Brown assured the boys there were only two humans in the mine, but Alex feared he would find a hand or a leg, or even worse, an entire body.

The most difficult parts of the dig were between seams, and Alex sometimes had to bash his way through solid rock. It was painful, and the enhanced skin on his fists broke and bled. He would have to stop for a few seconds to allow the nanobots time to repair the damage before continuing on.

Approximately forty minutes into their mission, Alex changed back again, resulting in a powerful fart that sounded like a fog horn underwater. It was quite astonishing really, and Ian was regrettably too close to the blast zone when it happened.

"Oh! You could have warned me!" Ian rapidly flapped his wings to disperse the gas. Alex held his last mining bee in his hand.

"Last one?" asked Ian.

"Last one."

"Reddish says we're nearly there. One more should do it. If it doesn't, you can have mine."

"Thanks, mate."

Suddenly, the tunnel shook. Rossolington's colliery it seemed wasn't quite dead yet, and another part of the mine collapsed in on itself. The shockwave caused parts of the tunnel wall to fall down onto the boys. A large rock smashed into Alex's bee carrying hand, killing the insect and breaking Alex's hand at the wrist. He screamed out in pain.

The earth shook around Frank and Mike. The large ceiling rock above them shifted and dropped a little, stopping just a few inches above Frank's head. Mike didn't say a word. Frank leaned over and put two fingers against his friend's throat.

"Still alive," said Frank.

The air around Frank was thick with coal dust. He checked his air tank; it was almost empty. The light from his torch was dimming, as was Mike's. *I'm a fool*, thought Frank.

"We should have saved your torch, Mike. But I guess it doesn't matter now."

Both torches dimly pulsed the last bits of power from their batteries, and then died. The flow of air from Frank's tank stopped. He started to cough as the dust, methane, and carbon dioxide filled his lungs. Frank tried to hold his breath, but after a minute and a half, he couldn't hold it anymore. He gasped and coughed for air, but there was none. Frank couldn't hold his eyes open anymore. Above him he could hear a scratching sound, and for a moment he thought he heard his son, Alex, call out to him.

"Hi, son," said Frank.

There was darkness, and peace.

CHAPTER 28

Strange Waiting Room

Frank carefully opened his eyes and squinted at the tree framed blue sky above him. He had woken up on a sofa in the woods. As his eyes got accustomed to the light, he looked around. To his right were doors of varying styles and colours being used to create a wall, to his left he saw a beat up old dressing table. Frank looked at the sky and trees again, it was less confusing. *This must be the waiting room*, thought Frank.

"Get up, you bloody idiot!"

Strange, thought Frank. He'd occasionally wondered about the afterlife and pictured serene pink clouds and friendly people enjoying toga parties. Not the sound of Donald Brock calling him an idiot. He had often heard about the mysterious workings of the folks in charge of the beyond department, so figured this was some kind of test or memory echo. The last thing he remembered was being trapped a mile underground, with no oxygen or hope. So in a weird way, it made sense the first voice he'd hear while waiting for judgement would be that of the greedy fat-cat who had caused his death in the first place.

An order was an order, however, even if God was doing his best Donald impression, so Frank carefully shifted his position on the sofa and sat up. He scanned his surroundings again and immediately started to doubt his after-life theory. On the floor to his left was Mike, unconscious. Beyond Mike stood a large filing cabinet wrapped in some kind of hard shell that looked, at least a little, like cling film, only the film was made of some kind of organic material, and there was a lot of it. Next to the filing cabinet was Donald Brock, also wrapped in the organic cling film, with just a tiny opening exposing his face, which looked cross.

"Frank, get me out of this," ordered Donald.

Frank stood up, stepped over Mike, and walked over to Donald in his cocoon. He gave the organic cling film an experimental tap. "How did you get stuck in there? What is this stuff?"

"It was a huge spider."

"Really, a big spider?" Frank nodded a placating nod. "Sure it was, and this huge spider dragged you into the woods to wrap you up like this?"

"No, I found the kids who stole my filing cabinet and followed them here. The next thing I know this huge spider falls through the blue tarp there. After that, it's a bit fuzzy. I think the spider mooned me."

Frank saw the blue tarp on the floor next to Donald and tried not to think about what a mooning spider looked like. His attention then turned to the filing cabinet. "And this is the filing cabinet you're talking about?"

"Yes, please get me out of this. There's been an accident at the mine, I need to get over there."

"Yes, I know. I was in the new seam when it collapsed."

"You were? I thought you were away on business."

"I came back early and visited the new seam."

Frank started to claw at the material covering the cabinet. It was slightly sticky to the touch, but only as much as a used lint roller.

"Hey, that's private property," said Donald.

Frank didn't care, and once he got behind the top sections of the sticky casing, he was able to get his entire hand between the cabinet and outer shell. Pulling the rest away from the top drawer was easier after that, and as soon as he was able, Frank pulled open the first drawer and looked inside.

"Frank! Leave it be. Those are private company files," said Donald.

Frank still didn't care. He started to scan the folder labels inside. He'd always suspected Donald was up to no good at the mine; he constantly increased quotas and frequently tried to dance around Frank's attempts to make the mine a safe place to work. This was a golden opportunity and Frank wasn't about to let it slip by.

"What's this?" Frank asked no one in particular.

He pulled out a folder labelled "Coal Train."

"What's coal train, I wonder." Frank scanned the documents inside.

"Now listen, Frank. It's just a little side project. I can totally let you in on it if you like. Want a new car? Done. Take the wife and kids on holiday? No problem, I hear the South of France is lovely this time of year."

"No, thanks," groaned Mike.

Both men turned their attention to Mike lying on the floor. Mike attempted to sit up against the sofa and winced as his ankle refused to cooperate. Frank put down the file folder and helped him.

"How do you feel, Mike?"

"Like I died but instead of heaven I ended up in a room with you two," said Mike.

"Take it easy, your ankle is probably broken."

"How did I—we—get here?"

"Your guess is as good as mine. But it has actually proven informative," said Frank.

Frank was curious about how they had managed to escape the mine and end up in a makeshift den in the woods. He wondered how both Donald and his precious paperwork ended up here too. Frank put those thoughts aside and turned back to the file folder he was reading. "It seems Mr. Brock here was helping himself and some friends stock up on extra coal. All the wealthy big wigs in the area too. Not by name, of course, but I recognize the addresses. Paying half the usual rate directly to Donald."

"Listen, lads," said Donald, as he shifted nervously inside his pod, causing it to wobble. "It was just a little off the top. Everyone was getting paid overtime on the new seam. Mike here was going to get a big bonus too."

Frank saw Mike look away in shame. He stepped over to Donald and put his face right up against Donald's little view port.

"Donald, shut your pie-hole. Your little deal here nearly got Mike and me killed, and the mine is likely gone for good. You are going away for a very long time."

Frank picked up a piece of the organic material he pulled off the cabinet and stuck it over Donald's peep hole.

"Right, we've got to get an ambulance for you, Mike and the police for this joker."

Mike pointed at the dressing table. "This den has a phone."

CHAPTER 29

New Rossolington

It was Friday, 6:30 a.m. Alex's alarm clock loudly announced the time, "it's 6:30 a.m., time to get up! It's 6:30 a.m., time to get up!" Alex slapped the tiny orange button on top of the cube-shaped digital alarm clock to shut it up. He listened for signs of life around the house, but couldn't hear anything. The Adams family morning routine would likely be different from now on.

It wasn't too long, though, before Alex's mum headed downstairs to fix breakfast, while Alex, Graham, and Robert battled for bathroom supremacy. Alex could hear his dad snoring in the master bedroom, enjoying a well-earned sleep-in after the pit explosion the day before. Alex, as usual, didn't sit for breakfast and grabbed a couple of slices of toast to-go. He walked over to Ian's house. They had a goodbye to make.

"So, who's sending me back?" asked Administrator Reddish Brown.

Alex glanced at Ian, who sported the self-satisfied look of a kid who had done all his chores already. Ian had had the pleasure of sending back Infected Yellow and the rest of the Secti days ago. Alex sighed. "Me, I guess."

"Very good. Just remember, deep breaths as I slide down your throat. We don't want a repeat of Ian's efforts the last time we tried this," said Reddish.

Alex recalled their first attempt to send the Secti back to the Nest. Eating tiny bugs, even the scary ones inside vitamin capsules was difficult enough, but swallowing a gob-stopper-sized piece of metal was no picnic. Ian had gagged and spat the Secti out several times before Infected Yellow got tired of it and physically forced Ian's tongue to lay still as the other Secti slid down his throat to the waiting portal.

"You have the list of insects we'd like you to send," said Reddish. "I'd still like you to reconsider that large creature with the massive mandibles."

"You're kidding, right? The stag beetle?" asked Ian.

Alex shuddered at the thought of trying to eat one of those scary insects. "Perhaps that one can wait for when you get back to build your own portal. Ready to go?"

At that point there came a tapping at the window. On the ledge outside, hopping back and forth, was Reddish's pet robin.

"I think someone else wants to say goodbye, Reddish," said Alex.

"Oh dear, I thought I had lost her. Could you boys perhaps do me a favour?"

"Sure, Red. What?" asked Ian.

"Could you feed her, please? She mainly likes worms, but sometimes she has a preference for ladybirds."

The thought of the mighty Administrator Reddish Brown, a super advanced robot lifeform from a distant planet, getting sappy over a little robin redbreast made Alex smile. "Sure Red, no problem. But I think she needs to go on a diet. I don't think robins are meant to be that round."

Reddish jumped down from the Secti-hacked transistor radio, and approached the two boys. "Thank you for your help. Visiting this world has been a fascinating experience. I'm encouraged by how much you've learned after your adventures. Remember, with great power —"

Alex grabbed Reddish Brown and tossed him into the air. As he fell, Alex positioned his mouth underneath the tiny robot, and plop, the visiting alien robot fell down Alex's throat and onward to The Nest. "Yeah, enough with the speeches."

"Wasn't that a bit rude?" asked Ian.

"Probably. It's not like we're never going to see him again."

Alex and Ian, also known as the Bug Boys, grabbed their school bags and left Ian's bedroom. Ian said goodbye to his dad and the two boys started their short walk to school. Heading into Oxford street, they were joined by Darren, who was sporting a new school uniform and less intimidating shoes. As the boys got to the end of Oxford street, they noticed something different. Among the other kids arriving at school were unemployed miners. With nothing better to do, they'd clearly decided to take a stroll with the kids to get some fresh air. Alex saw them huddled in groups near the entrance, probably talking about the future of Rossolington's colliery or where they might look for work. The days ahead were going to be tough for this little village after the pit explosion. It was all the news could talk about. The mine collapse, the ongoing scandal with Mr. Brock, and the local rich folk caught with massive sheds filled with coal. The strange tunnel behind the mine that appeared out of nowhere, and how Alex's dad and his friend Mike were able to get out. Alex was thankful the more pressing financial future of the village was getting more attention. The Bug Boys superhero game would have to be put on hold for the time being until everything calmed down.

Suddenly, a thought struck Alex. "Ian, do you remember when my dad gave us his lunch?"

"Yeah, best apple I ever had. I guess now we know why."

"That's it. Have you ever wondered what happened to the other apple?"

Acknowledgements

Several good people can be blamed for this book's existence! So if for some reason you were not entirely satisfied by my first attempt at novel writing, here's a list of people you can grumble about. They told me it was worth printing, so I did.

First, my readers, Edwin, Liza, John, Esther, Craig, Joe, Becky and Kaitlyn—your comments, suggestions, and support, helped push this project forward. Second, I'd like to thank the folks at the South Orange County Writing Critique Group, as those intense and honest discussions about this project really helped me shape it into something worthy of a bookshelf (I think).

A big thank you to my editor, Cindy Jewkes, for taking that all important fine-tooth comb to my manuscript, and the folks at iUniverse.com for getting it published.

Lastly, huge props to my friends and great writers in their own right who have been with this project from the beginning, Amanda and Alana. Thanks for keeping me motivated, and waving a red flag every time I wrote something completely stupid!

37655279R00111

Made in the USA
San Bernardino, CA
01 June 2019